C000185125

Bodach the Badger

By the same author

STRING LUG THE FOX

Bodach the Badger

DAVID STEPHEN

CENTURY PUBLISHING
LONDON

First published in Great Britain in 1983 by
Century Publishing Co. Ltd
76 Old Compton Street, London WIV 5PA

ISBN 0 7126 0176 7

Photoset in Great Britain by
Rowland Phototypesetting Ltd, Bury St Edmunds, Suffolk
and printed by St Edmundsbury Press,
Bury St Edmunds, Suffolk

For Kathleen
who cares about wildlife

Chapter One

It was cubbing time at the badger sett in the wooded glen below Ben Dearg, although the snow still lay deep in the high corries and gusted like a white sandstorm before the scourging wind on the tops. Up there the great crags and rock pinnacles were castles of ice, with gleaming battlements: every cascade was silent, the falling or spouting waters frozen to mushrooms and pillars that glowed with rainbow fire in the sun. For the sun was there in a gelid sky, probing with golden dirks between the storm waves of spindrift.

Countless generations of badger cubs had been born in the glen, on the rocky slope in the oakwood above the Breac burn: the Brook of the Trout. It was a quiet, lonely place – haunt of roe and squirrel, jay and blackcock – hardly visited except by the shepherd looking for a lost ewe or lamb, or by the stalker and his terriers out foxing in the spring. The age or depth of the sett no man knew, for it was old as place names are old, or the legends that go with them. In days long gone the Breac brocks had hearkened to the faint, far skirl of the Highland war pipes –

7

now an echo, like the wolf's howl, down the corridors of history.

In the glen the morning sun was warm and Bodach, the old boar badger, king of the sett, was lying in a grassy hollow, clear of snow, sucking a forepaw and sunning himself out of the wind. Night hunter though he was, born of a line that had prowled by night since before the coming of Man, he liked the feel of the sun, and in that quiet stronghold he could afford the risk of such a luxury. Now and again he would sit upright, like a bear, and claw chest and armpits with his foreclaws, blinking his eyes and licking his lips with obvious signs of pleasure.

The sett was under the oaks, above a great buttress of rock rising steeply from the burn. There the wind was always slight and the sun's rays warm. The crowded oaks – moss-grown, lichened and arthritic – baffled the fury of the wildest winter gales, and their harvest of acorns, varying from year to year, was devoured by roe deer and squirrels, or carried away and buried uphill by jays. Red deer sheltered in the wood when the wind raked the tops with its icy talons, and the remaining snow was churned by their hooves, stained with their droppings, and scraped where they had rested or grazed.

Bodach removed his forepaw from his mouth, rolled on to a hip, and licked under an armpit. The skin was scuffed there, by a slip on a rock in the night, and the frost was pricking. The licking was soothing and Bodach closed his eyes. But not his ears; or his nose. Suddenly his striped head went up, high, darting from side to side like a snake's. Deer were running in the wood.

They came on through the trees in a rush, waywise on the steep, with thud and swish of hooves – knobbers, staggies and high-antlered harts – with nostrils flared and flanks heaving in growing panic. They surged up to the rocks near the sett, turned broadside to Bodach, and halted. In one movement they swung their heads and froze, breathing vapour, to face down-hill. Bodach was alert, but not alarmed: prepared to watch yet ready to bolt underground at any threat to himself.

Ten paces clear of the others, and behind them, a little

8

knobber turned to face his backtrail, with ears forward and nostrils sifting, and there are those who would say he was acting watchman for the herd. Bodach sat on his scut and blinked. Twenty-seven deer and one badger waited, motionless, for the space of ten heartbeats: the deer alarmed and uneasy, the badger watchful but unafraid. And there was a mighty rush of wings in the clearway above the sett.

Bodach crouched. The deer crashed away. An immense shadow flashed across the discoloured snow and the eagle was down – *swoosh*! And up – swoosh! At tree height he heeled over and came down again, and the deer broke in wild stampede from the wood. But the eagle was not swooping to the assault; he was flying to roost and rest. As the deer bounded away in a cloud of misted breath he lifted above the trees, to a great leaning rock as big as a shieling, and reached for it with feet like grappling irons. When his yellow, black-clawed talons secured their grip he folded his vast wings, and blinked his fierce hazel eyes. Below the rock were scattered many of his pellets and three of his breast feathers to betray it as one of his roosting places. The pellets were fat wads of indigestible material bocked up by him, and were composed of bones, feathers, hare fur or deer hair, according to what he had eaten before he bocked.

The eagle closed his eyes and lifted one set of talons into the feathers of his belly. Bodach crouched, muzzle on forepaws: motionless, still alert, but not suspicious. He knew the eagle and had no fear of him. He had seen him take wing from the rock in the chill of many dawns. But he could not be sure that only the eagle had alerted the deer. So he waited on, listening, smelling, looking, although his eyes were of little use to him in the strong sunlight. There was no movement on the churned and slotted snow. When a grey crow flapped down, to swagger over the scrapes and peck at dark, shiny deer droppings, Bodach knew there was no peril close at hand.

Relaxing, he turned on his seat, and shambled up through the boulder tips by well worn tracks to one of the entrances to the sett. The entrance was in shadow; facing away from the sun. Icicles, sharp as a roebuck's top tines and longer than Bodach's

9

scut, hung like upper teeth over the entrance. Bodach thrust through the icicles, breaking them off like dry twigs, and turned about. He scooped them away with a paw and squatted at the entrance with only his striped face showing. The mewing of a buzzard, the harsh yarring of crows, the *prukking* of ravens, were familiar sounds. He sucked a paw, and drowsed.

Behind him, deep into the bank, Mathair the sow badger was curled up with her three helpless cubs on a dry bed of bracken, hay and oak leaves. This bedding she had laboriously gathered in the wood and on the Breac flats, homing backwards with it along her well worn runways with each bundle clasped to her chest. Her activities were betrayed by the bits and pieces she lost along the trail: she lost other bits and pieces at the entrance and when she was dragging her load down the tunnel to her nursery.

Forty yards along the slope, in a deep chamber behind a massive rock, another sow badger was nursing two cubs. She was Caileag, two years old, and this was her first litter. In front of the entrance to her nest was a great mound of padded earth, with a mat of old bedding on top. Mathair had dug out a new nursery chamber, so there was no old bedding on her doorstep; Caileag had cleaned out an old nest and replaced the old bedding with new. The tell-tale signs were scattered on the mound and snagged in the roots at the entrance hole.

The galleries of the sett were long and tortuous. Besides the three adults it held two yearling badgers: a male and a female cub of the previous year. Of this small clan Bodach was chief, by virtue of age and prowess. At that time he was six years old.

The wind eddied into his nostrils in spent breaths, ruffling the grey hair of his back and bringing messages to his wet nose. One message brought him suddenly awake, grunting and releasing his paw. The smell was fox . . .

Over the rocks, still feathered with ice on the north side, came a big hill vixen, red of leg and long of jaw, with her tongue out and her brush down, hirpling along on three legs. Bodach could smell her heavy musky odour; he could also smell her blood. But it is unlikely that he realised that her left forepaw was a bloody stump throbbing more agonisingly than an aching tooth. The big vixen had that morning chewed herself from a gin set by the keeper beyond the boundary fence, and had left three toes and four nails behind. And now she was seeking refuge in the badger sett!

Bodach had no particular feelings about her. Foxes were part of his world, like the grey crows, the squirrels and the deer: he neither liked them nor disliked them, and he certainly had no fear of them. This vixen was a stranger to him, but he felt no hostility towards her, and when she crawled into the hole above him, leaving blood spots on the snow, he made no move to challenge her, or stop her.

Perhaps he realised she was wounded, although that is unlikely: it is even more unlikely that he realised she would be sought after by her arch enemy Man. He had had foxes in the sett before, and did not like their dirty habits, their way of cluttering up the tunnels with remnants of prey or leaving bits and pieces on the doorstep for the blowflies to buzz over. In the past, he had tolerated fox lodgers for a time, so long as they stayed out of his way, then driven them out with threatening jaws when they invaded his privacy. Yet, now, he seemed quite indifferent to the intrusion of a wounded vixen.

For some minutes after she had gone to ground Bodach sat swaying from side to side like a bear: then he went underground to join Mathair, whose nose had had no tidings of the vixen's visit.

The vixen crawled slowly down a side tunnel not being used by the badgers. It was really a clan graveyard, for many dead badgers had been walled-in there, carefully buried in side pockets dug by Bodach and his ancestors. Their bodies might lie undisturbed for years; then skulls and bones would appear on the mounds at the entrances, excavated by a new generation of badgers driving new tunnels, for badgers are forever digging. The vixen found an unlined chamber behind a column of rock and lay down there to lick her aching paw.

No badger came to her all that day, but she heard the clan leaving after dusk to hunt. Throughout the night she stayed in the sett, preoccupied with the ache in her foot. At first light she heard the sound of water running in a quick thaw and went out to lap. Her paw was swollen and throbbing and would not be soothed by her tongue. When dusk came she was still lying nose to flank, with the injured paw laid carefully on her muzzle and a current of pain shooting up her leg.

She spent the second night lying up, with neither food nor water. By mid-day the pain in her foot had lessened, but she was racked by the pangs of hunger. Her flanks dimpled and flickered: she, too, was about to become a mother. But how could she hope to hunt in her condition?

Such thoughts may not have occurred to her, but she certainly made no effort to strike out on her own when she left the sett. Instead, she took up the trail of Bodach and followed it. If she could not hunt for herself she would play jackal to the badger.

Bodach padded at bear gait right down to the bottom of the glen, where the red deer were scraping and grazing at a slow walk along the burnside flat. The frost was settling and the iron entering the snow. Stars winked icily in a sky dark as mole's fur. Above the north shoulder of Ben Dearg the Great Bear was standing tall: the snow-capped peak hid the Dragon's tail. Above the pines on the opposite steep Orion stalked, with Sirius at heel and the pack of Hunting Dogs casting behind. And, presently, as though disturbed by the Hunter, unseen geese flew high over the pines, gaggling like foxhounds as they airted towards the Pole Star.

In such weather the Breac badgers usually stayed at home or close to it, coming out only to scratch or make brief forays to stretch muscles or use latrines, thus nursing their strength instead of expending it on fruitless hunting. In the autumn Bodach had put on fat: now he was lean, and hungry. But not hungry enough to weaken himself for no return. Tonight he would go no farther than the head of the glen. So he followed the slashed and slotted lane ploughed by the deer in the snow, and the vixen, limping on three legs, followed him, keeping in touch with her nose.

The glen opened out into a vast, gently sloping area of cut-over forest, and red deer were feeding among the tree stumps and along the avenues of layered, weathered branches. White hares were feeding there, spectral shapes against the patchy white; but they were too fleet for Bodach and he ignored them. The vixen drooled at sight of them but she knew she had no hope of hunting hares for many nights to come.

The deer ignored Bodach as he sniffed along the swathes of layered branches, or clawed at them where they were through-grown and snagged with grass. He scraped out a few crawlies from the depths, but they were mere morsels and he swallowed more dirt than prey. Then he found the remains of a blackcock that had been killed by a peregrine, and squatted down to eat it, warning off the vixen with grunts and a clicking display of teeth. She made no move to interfere. She was content to wait.

Before long her patience was rewarded. Bodach found the entrance to a rabbit's nest, or stop, under a clutter of branches. He sniffed at the sealed entrance, scraped away a little of the padded soil, which was mixed with tell-tale rabbit fur, and satisfied himself there were rabbits inside. But he did not start to dig at the mouth of the stop.

Instead, he crashed into the foiling branches and started to claw them aside. When he had cleared a space in which he could manoeuvre he started to dig straight down. The frost crust delayed his tearing claws for only a moment, and soon soil and roots and pebbles were flying past his flank. He was digging a shaft right down to the rabbit's nest, which was a foot below the surface at the end of a three-feet burrow.

In a few minutes he had the nest exposed. Seconds later he was clawing the young rabbits, thin-furred and open-eyed, from their nest of hay and wool. The vixen sat by impassively while he was digging, but when he had scattered five young rabbits on the layered branches she moved in to mooch.

At first Bodach grunted at her like a pig; but once he had settled down, chewing on one rabbit while holding down two others with his foreclaws, he let her sneak in to filch the remaining pair. Snarling, she drew back, and bolted both

13

rabbits before Bodach had started on his second. The food was a godsend to her, for she could not have dug out the rabbits for herself. But, being a fox, and a hungry one, she wanted more.

Bodach, however, had had enough of her, and when he rose, grumbling and showing his teeth, she realised she had gone as far as she dared. Badgers she knew as supreme minders of their own business, ever ready for the peace conference and the quiet life; but she also knew what Bodach's lock-jaws, with their powerful teeth, could do if she roused him to fighting pitch. So, with a parting snarl, she turned away and limp-trotted, one-two-three-and-hop, back to the sett, leaving Bodach on his own for the rest of the night.

The night was still many badger hours away from first light but Bodach, coming across Mathair's scent at the top of the glen, stopped hunting and turned for home. Finding her scent was nothing new or significant: it was a nightly event. Like him he left her markers all over their range. But this scent was different, exciting, compelling – the scent that drives young boar badgers stravaiging far afield in spring: the scent of a sow in heat. Mathair had been ripening to it for several days: now she was at her peak and leaving her signs along her homeward trail.

When Bodach arrived at the sett she was seated at the entrance to her nest, having just been to her cubs, and he bounded to her, purring. She touched noses with him in greeting, grappled with him, straddled him, and set her scent on him. Now they began to chase each other, up and down and along the slope, crashing through the oaks, rearing in embrace, pawing each other and play-biting. At the end of the play chase Bodach stood by her, purring, and she presented her rear to him.

They coupled for a long time, not knotted like foxes but for as long as foxes stay knotted. Afterwards Mathair bolted to her tunnel and went belowground to her cubs. Bodach sat on for a while after she had gone, arcing his snout and listening, then padded down to the Breac to drink.

There he met the young boar on the uphill trail to the sett. Although he was only a callow yearling, too young to mate, Bodach rushed at him, bit him as though he were an intruding stranger, and hog-shouthered him from the trail. The young boar was taken completely by surprise, and when he tried again to take the trail to the sett Bodach turned him like a collie kepping sheep, and pushed him aside.

If he had persisted it is likely that Bodach would have mauled him, but he did not wait to test the old boar's mood, any more than he would have tried to test his strength. Instead, he bounded away downhill and across the Breac, to a hole under a fallen pine near the top of the glen, one of many outlying burrows dug by the badgers on their range.

Grumbling in his chest, Bodach hurried back uphill and along the slope to Caileag's tunnel. He looked in and purred, but the only response was the faint mewing of cubs: Caileag was not at home. Restless now, fired by the fever of mating and with no urge to rest, he shambled back to his own tunnel, looked in, pulled out, climbed to the one above, where the vixen was lying and entered it. She was in the dead end still, not in his way, so he turned left back to his own quarters, by-passed Mathair, and reappeared on his own doorstep. Then he left on the uphill trail through the oaks and disappeared.

At daybreak Caileag appeared on the uphill trail from the Breac, her white face nod-nodding in the ground gloom. Bodach was following her at a spring-footed trot. She went straight to her cubs, and all his purring at the entrance could not rouse her. So he went to his own tunnel, and sat in the entrance, facing out, until the sun came up. Then the white face withdrew.

The yearling sow was already abed. She had gone to ground while Bodach was driving away the young boar, and was in a nest near where Caileag had her cubs. Although Bodach knew she was there, he did not visit her. She would mate that spring, but her time was not yet.

Chapter Two

Night after night, for the next week, the vixen was Bodach's shadow. Although the swelling had gone from her paw, and the wound was healing, she still walked and trotted three-legged because of the pain when she put the foot down and the greater anguish when she stubbed it against rock or hidden stump. She would be a limper for the rest of her life . . .

Not once did she follow the younger badgers or the nursing sows: it was always Bodach. And Bodach never tried to drive her away. Of course, when he found food, he always warned her to back off, and she backed; and if there was not enough for two she had to go without. But when there was enough to spare he let her share – after he was finished. Or she had the leavings.

In this way she eked out a living, without putting on fat, for Bodach spent as much time in the wood digging for hyacinth bulbs as he did afield looking for rabbits or carrion or earthworms. On nights when he was digging bulbs she had usually to go to bed with an empty belly, for the woodmice were still too nimble for her to catch and she had difficulty even with the slow-moving voles which she had to snap up because she had yet to learn the art of the one-footed pounce. She caught only a few: and what are a few voles to a fox that requires the equivalent of twelve each day?

The thaw came suddenly, with bland winds and sagging clouds. The ice castles melted like wax models in fire; the mushrooms of frozen spray dissolved; the pillars collapsed and were carried away. The hill freshets broke free again, and there was water-song in the ditches and channels running full to the Breac and the Slainte: the salmon river on the far side of Ben Dearg.

Curlews and peewits could be heard again on the moor, and in the cut-over wood. Iolair the eagle and his mate Fior-eun were carrying heather and branches to their eyrie on the west face of Ben Dearg. Pruk the raven was carrying carrion mutton to his mate, Borb, on her nest behind a stunted rowan on a cliff ledge across the glen from the eagles' eyrie, where she was sitting close on five near-hatching eggs. Mountain hares, some blue-and-white and some still white, held spring revelry, chasing, kicking and leaping, on a rocky flat a thousand feet below the ptarmigan, who live on the roof of the world.

One night, after the low ground was clear of snow, Bodach went foraging uphill, into the open above the cut-over wood, and found the remains of a red deer hind, on which the ravens and crows had been feasting for days. Sickening with fluke she had lain down in a hollow, and been covered by a blanket of snow that became her shroud. When the snow melted the scavengers found her. Now fox and badger ate their fill of venison, and afterwards both drank thirstily. It was the stoutest meal the vixen had eaten for more than a week. But when she went back the following dusk, without Bodach, she found that the last eatings had been cleared by fox and raven, buzzard, crow and eagle.

Disgruntled she sniffed over the fleshless bones. Then her thoughts turned to Bodach, and she hirpled away to seek him in the glen. It was close on daybreak before she found him, shambling along the steep slope, with the fore-end of a hare in his jaws: the remains, or rather the unwanted half, of Iolair's prey. The eagle was perched on the big rock above the badger sett, with the haunch under his feet. Syne he would carry it to his mate Fior-eun, now sitting close on two eggs.

Bodach knew the sunrise was not far off, so he was carrying the prey to a spot nearer home where he could eat it under cover without worrying about his timetable. He had a strong objection to being caught far from home in full daylight. The vixen could not get near him. Time after time he stopped to grunt at her, flicking his striped arrow head at her, and she was too wise to force her attention on him. In a hollow, about two hundred yards from the sett, he finally stopped and lay down to eat his meal, for it is an ingrained badger habit not to take prey into the den.

When he had eaten all he could, he left the remains and hurried home at a shambling trot, the hair on his back rising and falling like the fleece of a sheep. The vixen at once snatched up the leavings, girning slit-eyed as she did so. All Bodach had left were the head and the fore part of the rib cage. The vixen carried the prey to her den and, having none of the badger's scruples, went to ground with it in her jaws.

If she had been fit enough to hunt and keep bringing prey into the sett it is probable that Bodach, in the end, would have driven her out, especially if she had begun to clutter and foul up the tunnels being used by the badgers. But before she could commit a second offence badgers and fox had more serious things to worry about.

Two mornings later Bodach was lying at the mouth of his tunnel, rump in and face out, listening to the small-talk of snow buntings moving through the wood on their way to the high ground where dwelt the ptarmigan, when he heard the ominous scrape of hobnailed boots on the rocks above, then the voices of men, followed by the harsh yapping of terriers. He turned about at once and shuffled along the tunnel to where the sow badger was lying with her cubs. There he faced about again to stand guard in front of the nursery. He guessed what was coming; and he knew how to deal with it.

Inside the sett the outside sounds were muted, but all the

18

badgers were hearing, and sensitive to the earth tremors caused by booted feet. The sows cuddled closer to their cubs. The vixen drew in behind her rock, trembling in fear and pain. She was ready to give birth to her cubs, and while she waited the first was born: a wet, black mite no bigger than a month-old rabbit that squeaked as soon as it was clear of the enclosing membrane. The vixen licked it, pawed it behind her, and crouched down to wait.

Above ground were the head stalker, the under stalker, the shepherd and two varminty terriers: a lean, much-scarred Border bitch called Tarf, and her son by a Lakeland dog. The dog was called Sionnach, which is Gaelic for fox, and he was new to the brulzie. The stalkers had no quarrel with the badgers, and were dubious about putting the terriers into the sett to bolt a fox. They knew what a roused badger, fighting for his life, could do to even the toughest small dog.

'She had to pick the badger den, of course!' grumbled Coll MacDonald, the head stalker. He was a Clanranald man from Moidart, and there was a gentleness in him.

'Well, there it is,' said the shepherd. 'It was pure chance I was spying down this way, and there she was on the rocks, sore foot and all. What d'you think, Coll?'

'She'll no trap, that's certain!' interjected Simon Fraser the under stalker. 'That fit's a the lesson she needs tae mak her leery o them.'

Coll clasped his stick in both hands, then put his chin on them, perturbed. He could hunt foxes with the best of them when he had to, which was every year at cubbing time; but he hated all unnecessary killing, and had never been known to use a gin trap. He liked badgers. But he also liked his terriers.

'If the brocks stay clear the dog might bolt her,' he said. 'But they'll have cubs, and I canna see them standing by idle if the dog takes the wrong road. God knows how many holes and corners there are doon there. Still, I suppose we'll have to try.'

'We're all jalousin it's a bitch fox in there,' said Fraser. 'It could be a dog fox maybe, no?'

'Unlikely,' said Coll. 'It has to be a vixen. I wish tae peace

19

she'd stayed with her toes on the other side where she belongs.'

'It's a bitch all right,' the shepherd said. 'I could see her tits when I spied her. This has to be the one Campbell trapped.' Campbell was the keeper on the next estate.

'Let's get started then,' Coll said.

He tied Sionnach to a tree, and slipped Tarf, who had a face like a vampire bat, with dark, bristling mask. Fearlessly she darted into the fox-hole, and the men posted themselves on the rocks, with shotguns at the ready.

Down below there was fear among the badgers, but no panic. The sows began digging frantically, to put earth and distance behind them and the dogs, gathering their cubs to the fore each time they scraped a spoilheap between their hindfeet. The young badgers dug too. But not Bodach. He crouched on the threshold of his mate's nursery, blocking the tunnel so that nothing could pass him. The vixen waited, hoping . . .

But she was unlucky. The terrier, knowing her business, found the direct route to her, by-passing the waiting badger. She moved warily, till the reek of fox was strong in her nostrils. And, presently, her frenzied barking came faint and muffled to the waiting men, telling them she had found her fox.

The vixen drew back hard against the wall of the tunnel, and presented her sharp muzzle to the dog. Her lips lifted, showing her long, sharp tusks. Tarf rushed at her, girning and chopping, but the vixen met her teeth to teeth, and cut her slash for slash. Blood appeared on the fox's mask, not all of it her own. Realising she couldn't get behind the fox Tarf crouched down, yapping harshly, trying to stampede her into some kind of forward move. But the vixen was cunning; she had been baited before. She was content to leave the offensive to the dog.

The terrier's frenzied yapping, faint though it was to the men, told them much. They guessed the vixen was cornered, but refusing to budge.

'We'll leave her a wee,' said Coll, who now realised that Tarf had only the fox to deal with.

For several minutes dog and fox faced each other: Tarf growling in her throat, the vixen mute. Tarf was experienced, tough as oak, and totally without fear. She wanted to kill the fox, or get behind her and drive her out. She knew that if she failed, either way, she would be called out and the men would stand by waiting for the vixen to bolt. Always volatile, and a terror when thwarted, she worked herself into such a pitch of fury that she darted, without subtlety, to the clinch.

The vixen's teeth opened the skin above her eye; they cut her ear; they clashed against her tusks. But, blind to the bites, and roused to recklessness, Tarf was in and under, gurrying through the vixen's ruff for her throat. Her teeth found skin, and gripped and closed. The vixen chop-chopped at her attacker's flank, raking the harsh hair with her tusks, but held as she was there was no way in which she could deliver a serious bite.

Probably she knew that the terrier's grip was fatal if she could not shake it off. And she could not retreat. So she pushed forward, taking Tarf with her. They fought along the tunnel: a locked, squirming mass of fur, with Tarf hanging on, growling through locked teeth as she worried. Presently they reached a wider part of the tunnel, where it forked off to the nest of Bodach's mate and cubs, and here the vixen had more room to move. In her blind rush for the open she threw the terrier against a sharp knuckle of rock. Tarf yelped, winded, when the rock stabbed her ribs, and was scraped from her hold. And the vixen was free.

But she did not bolt. She turned back. As Tarf recovered another shape blocked the fork in the tunnel: a badger! It was Bodach, filling the tunnel with his bulk, standing there with head lowered, waiting . . .

For what? For the fox? No, not for the fox, for he let the vixen squeeze past him without demur. In fact, he drew in his bulk to let her through. He was waiting for the terrier!

Game though she was, Tarf was no match for the big boar badger of Breac, especially in her weakened state. Yet she shaped up to Bodach, bristling and snarling, with teeth bared to the gums: a brave fighter meeting another brave fighter with all the advantages of size and place on the badger's side.

At the first clash, Tarf's jaws gathered nothing more than

21

grey hair from Bodach's shoulder; but his teeth tore skin and flesh from her neck, and her howling was heard by the men at the den mouth outside. For a moment they couldn't understand what was happening. Then they saw the vixen at the entrance and they knew Tarf was face to face with a badger. Fraser shot the vixen as she bolted, then Coll was shouting:

'She's on to a badger! And maybe behind it, whatever. Turn Sionnach loose. Quick!'

He grabbed Sionnach when the shepherd turned him loose, and held him. 'Haud on for a minute. Take your time, dammit!' With the terrier oxtered Coll put his face to the hole and called: 'Tarf! Tarf! Come to me, d'ye hear? Here, girl, here! Tarf!' But Tarf did not come. He slipped Sionnach and rose to his feet.

'Hell, damn and blast!' he said to the others. 'She must be taking a pasting down there!'

'You'd been better tae trap her, or pooshen her,' the shepherd said.

'I should hae sat up for her and shot her,' said Coll.

Sionnach knew what was expected of him and needed no encouragement. He rushed into the hole, and down, hurrying to the help of the kennel mate who was his mother. And, because of the position Bodach and Tarf were now in, he came up behind the badger.

Now a badger's hide is thick and tough, armoured with hair, and the teeth of a terrier do not make much impression on it. And the working end of him – bone-splintering teeth and jaws like a trap – is enough to daunt the most dauntless terrier. But there is one part of him that a badger is sensitive about, a part he doesn't like touched – his scut. Bodach was no exception. So when he felt Sionnach's teeth at his tail he clawed the roof of the tunnel in a turnabout to face him.

And that let Tarf free.

Sionnach backed away when Bodach came breinging at him with upper lip curled and teeth clicking. But the badger now had two terriers to deal with, and no sooner was he engaged in a teeth to teeth brulzie with Sionnach than he felt other teeth at his scut. So he kept thrusting forward, forcing Sionnach back, knowing there was a sleeping nest ahead where he could make a half turn and get them both in front of him. That was his intention; but the experienced Tarf knew they had him at a disadvantage and meant to keep him there. Although she was cut about the face, and losing blood from her neck wound, she had no thought of quitting.

While Sionnach, in front, was biting and being bitten, Tarf kept worrying at his scut. But it couldn't last. Bodach turned about again, suddenly realising that he could rush Tarf to the dead end of the tunnel where the vixen had been lying, and worry her there. He swept her before him, irresistibly, ignoring the teeth chopping at his face. And it seemed that, at last, the ramgumptious little terrier must die down there, deep under the oakwood. But there was still her son: Sionnach!

As if understanding the badger's intention Sionnach mounted his rump, worrying and biting, then squirmed forward to slash at ears. The attack stopped Bodach, and he crouched low with his nose tucked into his chest. For the first time in his life he was being worsted. So he turned about yet again to deal with the attacker at his back. In that instant Tarf rushed at his flank and, whether by accident or design, Sionnach squeezed past him to join her at the front.

The dogs were now assured of a line of retreat; the exit was at their backs, and they could see the light. It was well for them that this was so, for Bodach now had them where he wanted them – in front. With his rear secure, he kept inching towards them, striking right and left with the speed of a viper, forcing them to yield ground or run the risk of a broken jaw: or worse. The terriers yapped and snarled, but they kept backing off, for they had no way of getting round Bodach's guard, and they now knew from experience the terrible punishing power of his teeth.

As they neared the mouth of the tunnel Bodach speeded up his attack, carrying the fight right to the dogs, as though he meant to kill them. More likely he merely wanted rid of them. The first inkling the waiting men had of the truth was when the terriers came out backwards, closely followed by a giant boar badger reaching for their throats.

Coll instantly called off the dogs. They came bellying up to him reluctantly, bristling like hedgehogs, with teeth bared to the gums. The stalker swore when he saw how his dogs were cut up, then turned to where Bodach was crouching, watching, with chin up, blinking his small dark eyes.

'Don't shoot him!' he roared to Fraser, who had raised his gun. Then he turned to the crouching badger. 'Take that, you auld scunner, you!' he said, and booted Bodach on the rump. 'Now get tae hell out of it!'

Bodach blinked, and kept moving. He shambled into his tunnel, suddenly aware of the perilous proximity of men. Their presence frightened him as no number of dogs could do.

'What now?' Fraser asked, without waiting for an answer. He lifted the vixen by the brush, tailed her with his gralloching knife, and stuffed it in his game bag for the bounty. The body he threw down the slope, where it rolled and upended grotesquely before lodging against a rock.

Coll was bandaging Tarf's neck with a big handkerchief, which he secured with a safety pin he took from under the lapel of his tweed jacket. The terrier, still brimming with smeddum, wagged her tail and licked his face, while Sionnach leaped at him, eager to be noticed. Coll patted him and roughed him over with affection.

'Yes,' he said to them, 'you're baith grand wee dogs when your wild's up.' Then he spoke to Fraser.

'I'm taking the dogs home, Simon,' he told him. 'You chaps carry on to the Piper's Cairn to see can you find a fox den there. But I'll tell you one thing, Simon, for sure. Nae dog of mine will ever gang into a badger sett again, fox or no fox! No! Not for God or Mammon!'

He put Tarf in his game bag and slung it round his neck, then started down along a deer trail to the Breac, with Sionnach leaping at him to his waist.

'You're for the walk home my lad,' Coll said to him. 'Your mither's sairer hurted than you.''

For some hours afterwards the badgers lay up, not sleeping, but taut and trembling, as though expecting another visit from the dogs. When Bodach realised they were not coming back he moved to his own sleeping nest, where he curled up to lick his fur and claw gently at the ear Sionnach had notched. There was clotted blood on it and the throbbing of it irked him. Mathair sighed and stirred, disturbing her cubs; they squeaked and began to nurse.

At darkening she poked her face from the sett, at the entrance used by Bodach. This was later than her usual time: the Breac badgers rarely waited for sunset before coming out. But Mathair was uneasy. The fear born in her that day was still with her, and she had lain long in the tunnel, listening and sniffing, before venturing to show her face. Her fear would pass: the cause of it she would never forget.

Warily she pushed her head out, the white of her face stark in the gloaming, listening with one ear to one side and with the other ear to the other; then she arced her nose across the wind – sniffing, sifting, savouring, questioning. Not only was her nose good: it was highly selective, able to pick out any thread of scent in a web of scents. Her eyes could be fooled, but never her nose, or her ears.

All her nose could own tonight was a nuance of red deer. Then a roebuck came upwind and minced past. He was in full antler, clear of velvet, with top tines like ivory dirks. The smell of him came back to her on the wind, not troubling her. She pushed her head right out, listened and sniffed for perhaps half a minute, then thrust clear to the shoulders. She pulled all of her back in again; then out and in and out again: thus she betrayed her unease. When, at last, she did come right out, she left at speed, her grey back thatch heaving like the fleece of a sheep. That was her fear of ambush. Across the Breac she slowed to a bear-walk: now she could forage. Some time in the night she would return to suckle her cubs.

Caileag came out next, circumspectly by habit, but without fear: although she knew there had been a disturbance she had not been involved with the terriers. She followed the trail taken by Mathair, and would probably hunt over the same ground. Last out was the yearling sow. After asking a few questions with her nose she took the uphill trail, aslant the slope and through the oaks to the open. There she forked left in the direction of Drochaid Farm.

And that left Bodach. A tawny owl hooted from a tree down the glen: an answering *kee-wick* came from his mate in another tree, where she was sitting on three eggs in the old nest of a crow, and ready to lay her fourth. Two hoodie crows were grumbling at roost across the Breac, rocking flat-footed on high pine branches, trying to sleep. A woodcock flew across the open lane of sky, slow-flapping at deceptive speed, and at that moment Bodach's face appeared at the entrance from which he had driven the terriers.

His ear was thick and *ticking*, distracting him; but not enough to divert it or his nose from their business of asking questions. His nose could own the scent of the roebuck Mathair had seen passing by earlier; his ears hearkened to the whisper of leafless, trembling oaks, and the wind flaffs running like mice feet in the old ferns on the slope – all meaningful but harmless sounds. No hint of danger came to his ears or nose.

Satisfied, he came out on to the mound of earth at the entrance, and sat down to scratch his flanks, whimpering when his claws touched his *ticking* ear. Next he sat up like a bear to claw his chest and armpits. Then it was time for him to go, and he took the well-worn trail up past the eagle's rock.

Chapter Three

The wheatears arrived while the last of the snow, printed by the feet of hares and ptarmigan, still lay in high hollows and gullies on Ben Dearg: on the lower spurs and ridges Blackface sheep were paunching on the first green blades of moor grass. Red grouse were astir in the heather, muttering and chuckling in their throats. Mahogany cocks, with scarlet combs, and legs wrapped in ermine, leaped and crowed, calling *Go-back; Go-back; Go-back!* from commanding hummocks and lichened boulders. The red deer had moved to higher ground, in hind groups and stag groups: the strongest stags in early velvet, the less fit still wearing their old antlers.

Iolair the eagle was hunting hares, grouse and rabbits for his mate Fior-eun, now sitting close on two eggs. The ravens Pruk and Borb were feeding five near-fledged young, red-gaped, and dandruffed with pickings from their quill sheaths. The old ravens had a sure source of food near the nest: the carcass of a sheep uncovered by the melting snow. Larks were singing, curlews calling, and the keening of peewits was heard by the badgers far into the night.

Ring ouzels, the blackbirds of the mountains, were back on the hill, and willow warblers in the oakwood, before the Breac badger cubs appeared above ground for the first time. They came out timidly, their ears and noses awed by this new world with its strange sounds and smells, and hardly strayed from their doorstep until Mathair appeared. She suckled them, and played with them for a brief spell, then she shook them off and left them, taking the downhill trail. The cubs made no move to follow her.

Minutes later Bodach appeared and sat down to scratch, his hindfoot thudding when it grounded after each claw-stroke. Hearing him, the cubs ran to him, jumping and squeaking, eager to fuss; but he brushed them aside, not roughly, and padded away without stealth on the uphill trail – a giant of his kind; broad of chest, sheathed in muscle; hen-toed and out at elbow; bear-like, with the bear's inswinging gait. In the gloom under the oaks only the white of his face was visible: a weaving, disembodied whiteness no darkness could conceal.

Up and up, past Iolair's crag, the white face bobbed and flickered, as Bodach followed the windings of the well-trodden trail. His face markings, like the skunk's black and white stripes, were a warning, flashing danger signals ahead of what was following on. *Stand aside!* they warned. *Molest me at your peril!* But there was nothing ahead to take note, except a roebuck, and he had no cause to be alarmed. He knew Bodach, and Bodach knew him, and they had never shown more than recognition interest in each other.

The buck faced about as the badger approached, and was in time to see him porpoising past, for Bodach had changed pace and was bounding now, like the giant weasel he was. The wind was a siren's song and he was answering. At the top of the slope, where the trail forked, Caileag was casting about, trying to unravel the tangle of scent lines left by young rabbits that had grazed and played there earlier. Bodach touched noses with her. Her greeting was friendly, so he began purring to her like a cat (he had what the stalker would have called a 'grand set of bagpipes'). Caileag was receptive, but not yet ready for mating, and ran away from him when he tried to mount her. After a clumsy attempt to persuade her to play Bodach left her, and shambled away along the left fork, which led to Drochaid Farm where there was a bridge across the Breac.

Two families of badger cubs were now alone at the sett, each unaware, as yet, that the other was anywhere near. Caileag's cubs were a week younger than Mathair's, so were even more timid, and tired more quickly. After half an hour they went below ground to await the return of their mother.

Mathair's cubs, despite their small size, were rough in their play, grappling and leaping at each other, rolling over in close embrace, falling head over heels in threesome, squeaking, yelping and biting. One cub found a frog, which all three tried to scoop up with a paw, but they lost it when it leaped downhill. The more excited they became the more noise they made, and the tawny owl heaving half asleep on her owlets in her nest across the Breac, turned her head twice to stare in their direction with her dark, lustrous eyes. Then she forgot about them.

Neither family knew about the man seated fourteen feet up in a stag-headed oak midway between the cub-holes: nor could they smell the smoke from his pipe because it was drifting high overhead across the burn. Mathair had no suspicions when she passed under the drift scent of man and tobacco on her downhill trail. Bodach and Caileag had missed them, being upwind from the moment they left the sett.

Coll MacDonald had chosen the night and his high seat well, knowing before he left his cottage that the wind would be in his favour. He had approached the sett from the burn, and been on his seat since an hour before sunset. He was an observant man, with an inquiring mind, who believed that if you wanted to know more about an animal you should go out and look at it. The encounter between Bodach and his terriers had stirred his interest in the badger clan and he wanted to know more. Being an experienced stalker he had long ago learned about the vagaries of wind and scent, so he knew how to set himself up for badgers although he had never done so before.

29

The night grew chill, with the wind becoming restless, and eddying, but Coll knew he was safe so long as it did not change direction. He pressed his tweed two-snooter firmly down on his head, and pulled the parka up round his ears. When Mathair's cubs at last became tired and went back into the sett he thought of giving up for the night; but the thrawn bit was in him, as they say, so he waited on, rubbing his hands and twiddling his toes, with his head full of questions. Would the sow stay away till morning, or would she come back in the night to her cubs? Would the cubs come out again? He decided to stay on till the howdumdeid (midnight is the English of it: the Gaelic is *meadhon-oidhche*).

He was glad he had done so, for presently Mathair appeared on the trail below, padding uphill purposefully, clearly in a hurry, her white face bobbing in the dark like a dancing highlight, and Coll was reminded of the way a horse tosses and shakes its head when pulling a load or when being tormented by flies.

The wind was still steady and Mathair came on, totally unaware of the presence of the man. She came right up to the sett, thrust her face in at the tunnel entrance, and purred: a summons to her cubs that Coll could not hear. But he guessed she had called them, because they came storming out and rushed at her in a booroch, yikkering, and yelping like very small puppies, hustling her till she stood for them. When the white flickers of faces disappeared Coll surmised that she was suckling them, and when they appeared again he guessed that she had shaken them off. What happened next was not clear to him because he was too far away.

Mathair stood back from them, then turned about and slouched away down her own back trail. The cubs bunched together, in a close circle, heads to centre. They were eating. Mathair had bocked up food for them. The vomit was warm and steaming, and the cubs ate it greedily: pulped earthworms, beetles, slugs, woodlice, a vole, and a hedgehog, complete with four quills accidentally swallowed. After eating the vomit the cubs began to play, making more noise than before. Coll had no idea how long they would play, and decided it was time for him to go.

But he was cautious, and not until he was as sure as he could be that Mathair was well away did he climb down from the oak tree, his South Uist tweeds and felt boots making no more noise than a fox. At the bottom of the tree he sat down to look and listen; then he palmed his way down the slope on his seat (bumming his way down as said later) in case he might offer the cubs a silhouette if he stood up. On the bank of the Breac he pulled his whisky flask from the inside pocket of his jacket, and gulped a mouthful of the Glenlivet – from the very place itself.

Homeward bound he was; but he turned away from the homeward trail. He got down on his hands and knees and began to stalk back up the slope. He wanted closer to the cubs than he had been earlier, and was sure he could do it because the wind was blowing from the sett on to his face. On the stalk he made no noise, placing hands and knees carefully and firmly as he crawled, pressing down frush fern stems that were in the way, lifting and laying aside sticks that might snap under his weight. And, suddenly, he had the cubs in view at a distance of six yards: ragrowstering, yelping, squeaking, yikkering, leaping and falling over each other, not knowing he was there.

Lying on his stomach, with chin cupped in his hands, came easily to Coll: he was used to the long belly-crawl and the long wait when stalking red deer on the open hill. So he was prepared to stay with the cubs for what he would have called a whiley. But within minutes he thought he had lost them for the night. Sealgair the tawny owl flew over with a vole for his mate and owlets across the burn, and signalled his arrival with a wild war-whoop: *Kee-wick, kee-wick, kee-wick!* The cry was familiar to Coll, and his ears merely noted it; but it was a strange, menacing sound to the cubs, and they bolted underground before the third whoop.

'Damnation!' Coll said to himself under his breath, amazed that badger cubs, beasts of the dark, should be scared of an owl's cry. In fact, they had no idea what an owl was, or looked like. All sounds in the strange outside world were new to them, and at that stage they would have reacted in the same way to the yap of a fox, or the *bough* of a roebuck, or even the snapping of a twig. Naïf they were, but they would learn with experience; in the meantime the sett was their citadel, in which lay safety.

Sealgair flew away to hunt again, and Coll could hear the faint *wee-wicking* of the hen on the nest. Then she fell silent and began to feed her owlets, passing morsels of vole to them under her body without uncovering them. The badger cubs appeared, their fright forgotten, and resumed their play. Presently one of them broke off and, finding an eagle feather, scooped it with a paw. The wind blew the feather towards Coll, and the cub followed it. Coll pressed his chin to the ground, straining his eyes to look up from under the skip of his two-snooter. He was beginning to regret having stalked in so close.

The eagle feather was now lying within his reach. The cub pounced on it, and stopped, staring into the man's face. Coll stared back at it, unblinking, almost afraid to breathe. The cub knew he was there but not what he was, and its nose was telling it nothing because he was downwind. It came forward, arcing its snout, and sniff-walked past his right shoulder: it brushed against his hip, then walked over his feet. It came up on his left side and sniffed his cheek, touching it with its wet nose. Then it ran back to join the others in a play-brawl, the man and the eagle feather forgotten.

Coll swithered about backing away, but decided the cub needed a lesson. He would give it a fright (fleg it a wee was how the thought took words in his head) to teach it. He palmed up on his knees, looked at them, and said in a low voice: *Woof! Woof!* The cubs stopped playing and looked towards him, not seeing him and not smelling him, alerted but not alarmed. But when he jumped suddenly to his feet they fled, hearing only the first of his parting words to them: 'Ye'll hae tae be mair leery than this wi the mannie on the ither side or he'll hae your hides for sporrans.'

He hurried down the slope, with arms spread for balance, and digging in his heels to keep his feet. Across the burn he looked at his watch. It was half an hour from the howdumdeid . . .

32

Coll was in his bed when Bodach forced his way under the bottom wire of the fence into the big pasture at Drochaid Farm, where a Shorthorn bull was running with fifteen cross-Highland cows and heifers, some with calves at foot. The cows lifted their heads to stare at him; the bull rose ponderously from his cudding and wheeled to watch him on his way. Two near calving heifers followed him, snorting, with heads down and tails up, then lost interest in him when he began turning over old, hard-skinned dung pats in search of earthworms. From old pat to old pat he weaved about the field at a swinging trot, ignoring fresh dung and hardly noticing the grazing cattle.

The cattle were still being fed hay, laid out along the inside of the bottom fence, and Bodach nosed and scraped where it had been trampled into the soft ground. He followed the fence line, still nosing and scraping, sitting up every now and again in listening attitude, as stoats and weasels do. Near the top of the field two cows were lying chewing cud. They rose when he passed between them, and one followed him to the fence, with head lowered in half threat, turning back when he pushed under the bottom wire.

There was a narrow ride along the length of the fence, and across it a larch wood netted against rabbits. The ride was hummocky with heather and blaeberries, through which seedling birches were leafing: foxgloves, tall as the red deer on the hill, grew there in summer, their bells sagging and shaking under the weight of fat, furry bees.

Bodach followed his own well trodden trail across the ride to the netted fence, and pushed into the larch wood through a heavy swing gate covering an entry just big enough to admit a badger. The gate closed behind him. It had been put there by the forester to let badgers come and go, after they had clawed a hole in the netting or torn it up from the bottom, giving rabbits a way through a fence that was supposed to keep them out. Now the fence was intact, and the gate that let the badgers in and out barred the way to rabbits.

Drainage ditches flanked the trail through the wood: only three, wider and deeper than the others, crossed it. The larches,

33

now roe height, screened it. Bodach plodded along without haste, swinging his head left and right, bear-like, his ears and nose alert. In a grass tussock, on the edge of the right hand ditch, he heard a rustle, and there pinned down and killed a field vole, which squeaked once before he swallowed it whole.

The trail led to another gate in the fence near the top of the cut-over wood, and Bodach pushed through without pause. A short-eared owl, surprised while standing on a vole, rose almost at his feet and flapped away, taking the vole with her in her claws. Leaving the trail Bodach followed the top of the slope, above the last line of layered branches, and was himself taken by surprise when a mountain leveret came running at him, flat-eared and at speed, with a big dog fox coursing it and gaining ground. The leveret almost crashed into him, but his reflexes were slow, and it jinked past him untouched by paw-stroke or snapping jaws.

The fox, taken aback, checked when he saw the badger, trotted a few paces, then swerved past him in full stride. By then the leveret was in a peat hole behind a low knoll, head in and rump out, its ears flat and its flanks trembling with fear. Unlike the brown hare of the glens and straths, the mountain hare will sometimes go to ground, in burrow or under peat overhang, when hard pressed or during storms of rain or snow. The fox tracked the leveret unerringly to its hiding place, and was digging at the hole when Bodach bounded into the cut-over wood. He had it out, and dead in his jaws, before the badger reached the old drag road at the bottom end.

Across the drag road stood a shed of unweathered larch, with roof of corrugated asbestos, that had been put up as stabling for the big, gentle Clydesdale horses that had drawn the timber when the wood was being felled. Woodmice haunted it: two swallows newly arrived were roosting in it beside an old nest of the previous summer. In it Bodach killed a woodmouse, which he caught under the heck used for hay, and bolted it where he stood. He was hungry: a vole and a woodmouse and some earthworms were scant prey for the biggest boar badger on the forest of Dalnabreac. But he also wanted to rest, so he curled up under the heck, on a bed of wood shavings and old hay, and fell asleep nose to flank. And syne the swallows could hear the deep breathing of him.

When he awoke the wind was freshening from the southwest: the night was starlit but moonless. Bodach left the drag road and set off at a shambling trot across the open ground towards the head of Glen Breac. A peewit rose from her eggs and dived at him, screaming her alarm, then lifted away to be joined by her mate. Both birds began to chivvy him, swooping low over his head then throwing up on humming wings to swoop again; but Bodach plodded on stolidly, not hurrying, his white face bobbing in the dark. When he was off their territory they turned back, leaving him in peace. But not for long. A pair of curlews picked him up, one flying at his face from the nest, the other arriving to dive at him seconds after her cry of alarm. Then they, too, turned back when he had left their territory.

Sheep, near the lambing, trotted aside to give him passage, and stared after him till he was lost to view. Two white-faced stirks bolted, snorting, with tails in the air, when they saw the white front of him nod-nod-nodding at knee level towards them. He lapped water at the Breac before crossing, by way of flat stepping stones, without wetting his feet. Ahead of him was The Corrach, the ancient pinewood on the ridge above the Breac, with trees reaching down to the head of the glen, then up in a straggle to crest the high bank opposite the badgers' sett. Bodach sat down among the hazels on the edge of the wood to lick the soles of his feet and scratch his shoulder where a flea was biting. Then he sat up with forepaws across his chest, like a performing bear, with muzzle up-pointing and ears cocked.

'Tick . . . Tick . . . Tick.' The sound was like the ticking of a clock, followed by another like the popping of a cork. The sounds came from a knowe in the wood, where the trees opened into a clearing. To Bodach they were remembered sounds, not heard daily or nightly, or weekly, or monthly, but only for a short period each spring. Cock capercaillies were displaying in the wood.

Bodach elbowed his way through the hazels into The Cor-

35

rach, not to hunt capercaillies but because it was part of his range and he knew where he wanted to go. Before he reached the knowe he could smell the heavy musk of fox – a dog fox: perhaps the one he had met earlier. The fox was crouched among blaeberries behind the massive roots of a windfall – a pine two centuries old, with mossed, deeply fissured bark – waiting for a bird to parade close enough to be snatched. He had killed capercaillies before, and knew how unwary they could be on the ground.

The fox grimaced at the badger, but waited in ambush. Bodach shambled round the knowe, as yet unseen by the birds. One was parading close to the fox, with tail fanned, beard aggressively on end and beak pointing to the sky – a shadowy shape of eagle bulk: the biggest grouse in the world. He strutted and slow-walked, clicking his powerful beak, and *ticking*. Every now and again he would leap into the air like a blackcock, and Bodach could hear the *pop* and *squech* of him. Four other cocks were parading, posturing and challenging, but none came to blows. The display of the cock capercaillie is largely formalised posturing, like a heated debate in Parliament.

Bodach walked boldly on to the parade ground, without stealth, and the birds heard and saw him at once. All stopped strutting, and watched him: although less wary on the ground than in the trees they were not foolish enough to ignore a badger. Bodach padded on and the birds, like the sheep, drew aside to give him passage, their rivalries momentarily forgotten. And very likely that would have been the end of it: the badger going on his way and the birds returning to their display. But there was the fox . . .

Suddenly he rushed on to the knowe, with brush flying and teeth showing, keyed up for the kill and hoping to take the alerted birds by surprise. He almost succeeded because their attention was fixed on the badger. But he was too late. Three more strides and he would have had the nearest bird, but before he could reach it all five were in the air, rising with tremendous whistle and clatter of wings, then away into the dark, flap and glide, silently, in headlong high-speed flight. And that left the display ground to the fox and the badger.

Clashes between foxes and badgers are rare: when their paths cross they usually pay little heed to each other. But this dog fox, thwarted, and roused by failure, and perhaps seeing the badger as the cause, had a mind to fox-nonsense. So he pounced at the badger's rump – light-footed, taunting, snapping on air. Bodach was sniffing at downy feathers and droppings the size of walnuts when the teeth clicked at his scut, and that was enough to make fox business his business. With a speed surprising for his bulk he rushed at the fox – teeth bared and arrow-head darting like a snake's. Faced by twice his weight and those bone-breaking teeth the fox skipped out of the way, all fox-nonsense gone from his head. Cat-footed he trotted from the knowe, with a great show of indifference, leaving the display ground to the brumbling badger.

One capercaillie had returned and pitched in a pine tree before Bodach left the knowe. A layer of dark fuzzy cloud was creeping across the sky like a slow tide, blotting out the stars. The wind had died and the morning was growing warmer. Soon the first smir of rain was whispering in the pine tops. Bodach, plodding waywise through the wood, felt the gossamer touch of it on his face, and stopped to rub his eyes with a paw. The smir became a steady drizzle of fine rain, purring in blaeberry and juniper thickets, puddling on the needle carpet, and dripping from the trees. It soaked Bodach's face and back thatch but not his underfur, which remained dry. Under a squat pine with dense mushroom crown he stopped to shake the water from his fur, and the shaking quilled the hair on his face. There he saw Mathair crossing his back-trail at a spring-footed trot, homing on her second visit to her cubs. There was no greeting between them.

The rain became a smir again, then stopped, and Bodach left his shelter, veering right from his original course, but not on the trail of Mathair. He was heading for the ridge on the opposite side of the Breac. That way lay Drochaid Farm, with its cornfield, ploughland, pastures and hedgerows where, on such a morning, a badger might hope to find earthworms.

Bodach left The Corrach at the head of Glen Breac, climbed the ridge through thinning trees, and followed the pine hackle till he was opposite the sett. On the exposed flat of a grey stone he found Mathair's scent, a contact sign she had rubbed there from her anal gland. Bodach sat down and, with hindfeet off the ground, rubbed on his own scent beside it. Then he went to the nearby latrine she had used, and squatted over it. The latrine was a shallow pit dug by the badgers, and was half filled with soft dung like clay. Once they had filled it they would dig a new pit, leaving the old one uncovered.

From there Bodach took a little-used downhill trail to a small fir planting, leaving his five-clawed, hand-footed tracks where the wet soil was bared. Beyond the planting was an unmade road, rutted by tractors, which he followed to the Drochaid cornfield. In the cornfield the oats were brairded. An untrimmed hedge of thorn and dogrose separated it from an inbye pasture where five Aberdeen Angus cows were running with black calves at foot. In the cornfield peewits were nesting, some sitting on eggs and one brooding cheepers.

Bodach found earthworms along the cornfield endrigg, close to the hedgebottom, where he licked up slugs and beetles. In a hedgerow oak a tawny owl was flapping its wings, drying them out after being treed by the rain. The owl mewed *wee-wick* to the passing badger, and at that moment the exciting smell of rabbit came to Bodach's nose; not far away, and not going away. Indeed it was coming closer.

Rabbit snares were set along the bottom wire of the hedgerow fence, unknown to Drummond of Drochaird Farm, and in one of them a rabbit was strangling; kicking and somersaulting with the whites of its eyes bulging and pupils skellied. Bodach killed it, chewed it from the snare, and lay down under the hedge to eat it, leaving the head to the last and a few wisps of fur on the grass and wild liquorice. Then he started his endrigg prowl again to look for more earthworms. He could fast for a week at a time when prey was scarce; he could gorge himself when enough came his way.

The morning was grey-dark, and lights were on at the farm,

before he left the cornfield, meaning to cross the Breac by the hump-backed bridge. He squeezed under the bottom wire of the hedgerow fence, narrowly escaping putting his head in a snare, and was followed by the black cows and their calves to the farm road, where they stopped at a gate of birch poles, slung between strainers, and watched him spring-trot away. He crossed the road, circled wide round the farm buildings, and quickly reached the bridge. But his way was barred!

She was standing there like a canine Horatio – a callow black-and-white collie pup, a bareskin two-face, with a head full of brains and innocence, and play on her mind. She ran yapping to the badger, with her tail sweeping the ground, but the badger turned about and porpoised away. The last thing Bodach needed at that time of the morning was an argument with a dog in the open near farm buildings where the lights were on and people stirring.

So he bolted along his back-trail, with the dog following, yelping excitedly. He found a bank, undercut behind the exposed roots of a big beech tree, and into this he backed, hoping the dog would go away. But she came on, and danced about at the entrance, full of excitement, yelping playfully and wagging her tail. Bodach made threatening darts at her when she poked her face too near his refuge; but she would not be put off. In her innocence she had no idea what a dangerous game she was playing, and in the end she bellied down facing him, yapping from time to time, and keeping him on edge.

She held him there in the overcast half-dark until the sunless sunrise, and it was then Drummond missed her, and called: 'Nell! Nell! Come tae me!'

Nell rose and pricked her ears, wanting to go but not wanting because she was still hankering after the badger. Then Drummond whistled a shrill recall, and that was something she could not, and would not, ignore. Reluctantly she left and trotted away, with her feathered tail down-curved, casting longing looks behind.

Birds were singing when Bodach left the hole in the bank to go home by the way he had come. He turned off the ridge before

39

he reached the spot where Mathair had set her scent and bounded down on a diagonal towards the Breac, big-rumped and sure-footed, slithering and sclaffing where dips in the ground had become glidders of mud. The burnside flat was water-logged, and he had to high-step across, slowed to a walk. When he reached the burn his black legs were plastered with mud almost to the elbows. This was one of his routes when the burnside flats were dry, but that morning, with the light coming up, he was taking the shortest way home.

The water washed the mud from his legs and belly-fur as he splashed across to a sandy shoal under the opposite bank, where quivers of pinhead minnows poised and darted. They scattered from the tread of clawed hand-feet and were lost in the upswirl of sand; but they were back again when the cloudiness cleared, prodding steeply at badger tracks which the water soon smoothed over and filled again.

By then Bodach was halfway up and across the home slope, less than a minute from the sett, in a clearing where young thorns grew among old stumps overgrown with brambles. A woodcock, couched beside a windfall near the edge of the clearing, rose as he ducked into the underpass and flew owl-like away. Bodach shambled into the oakwood under an abacus of marble galls, and broke into a run. He ran over the entrance mound and into his tunnel. He was the last badger home.

Chapter Four

A queen wasp was working on a dead hazel stool below the
badger sett, rasping off a mouthful of rotted wood, pulping it in
her jaws, then carrying it to a mousehole in the oakwood above
the entrance to Caileag's nursery. Her paper nest, attached to
the roof of the burrow, was already the size of a walnut, with a
hole in the bottom by which she entered and left. One tier of
comb was complete, with grubs in the cells – the first generation
of worker-wasps-to-be.

The queen was in her mousehole when the bitch stoat
Fraioch came prospecting along the badger trail, nosing here,
querying there, whisking uphill and down, pad-pad-padding
then sitting tall to sniff and listen, displaying the snow white of
her chest and belly-fur: she was looking for a nesting place. The
mousehole attracted her, but when she poked her face into the
entrance she was confronted by the queen wasp crawling out
with a mouthful of soil. Instead of flattening her with a nimble
paw she stood aside, hissing, and let her fly away; then she
looked into the mousehole again. Her inspection was brief, and
she left to resume her search, perhaps because she realised how
much digging she would have to do to make a mousehole into a
nursery.

Fraioch was a yearling, born in May and mated in July: now she was ready to give birth to her first family. Stoats have a drawn-out pregnancy, with development of the young delayed for nine months after mating.

Glen Breac was new ground to Fraioch; she was from Ardcreag across the river. But she had left her old territory after her mate had been taken in a gin set by Colin Campbell the keeper – the mannie on the ither side as Coll MacDonald called him. Finding no stoat-sign in the oakwood she knew it was unoccupied territory where she could settle in peace. Her first choice of nest, under a mossed stump higher up in the oakwood, had been torn partly open by a fox and back there she would not be going.

Not far from Caileag's tunnel entrance was an unused hole in the bank, dug out by the yearling sow when she was a cub; not because she wanted it to live in but because badgers are forever digging. It was a dead-end burrow, three feet deep and Fraioch, after exploring it, was satisfied with it as a place for her nursery. Knowing her time was near she made haste to gather material for it.

She found a source among the hazels by the burn where the grass was dry and withered, and bit off tufts which she carried to the burrow in her mouth. All morning she fetched and carried, bounding downhill and up with her head held high, the tufts in her mouth looking like bushy whiskers. About the middle of the day she stalked and killed a baby rabbit, which was light enough for her to heft and carry to her den, although on the way uphill she trod several times on its hindfeet. She curled up with it among the bedding she had collected, ate part of it, then went to sleep.

In the late afternoon she came out to gather more hay, and when she had carried in enough to make her nest she hundled it all to the end of the burrow, ruffled it, trampled it, turned round and round in it and gathered the straggles about her, screening her face and eyes. Before lying down in it, and without stirring a paw, she reached out for the rabbit, long-necking, sniffed it over, snatched it in her teeth, and jerked it

42

into the nest beside her. She ate more of it, chewing noisily, and fell asleep, nose to flank, with her bushy tail over her face.

At sunset she was out again, casting about like a stoat unravelling a criss-cross of scent lines. She was looking for a place to use as a latrine, and found it under a big rowan tree, on a mound like a moleheap – the spoil from a shallow pit dug out by a badger cub many years before, and now hard packed and mossed over. On it she deposited two scats like withered broompods, black and shiny, with twisted whisker tips; they smelt of musk.

She was sniffing at them when Bodach suddenly appeared, coming towards her at a shambling trot. Startled she climbed into the tree, filling his nostrils with the musk smell of her fright. Although he saw the movement of her he could not see the shape of her, but he knew what she was because his nose recognised the taint of her. Having no special interest in stoats he padded on into the wood.

She was ready to come down when Mathair and Caileag appeared, so she stayed in the tree to wait until they had gone. But her time was not yet. Before they were out of sight Sealgair hooted his time signal and flew from his roosting tree to begin his night's hunting. The noise froze her, and the sight of him kept her frozen on her perch. Wisely, she was afraid of him, or of any winged predator his size. Although she was outside his normal prey range she might quickly come within it if he saw her, because he had five mouths to feed and one bitch stoat is the weight of eight voles. But he was hunting near the cut-over wood, where voles were swarming, so had no need to risk such dangerous prey and would probably have ignored her.

With Sealgair gone from the wood Fraioch started to climb down, but again she was forced to halt and stay where she was. The yearling sow badger reared from the ground not twenty yards away, and climbed on to the mound at the entrance to her tunnel, where she sat down to scratch herself, grunting when she clawed too vigorously at an ear. Then she plodded slowly along the slope below the sett and stopped to sniff at stoat scats before leaving on the downhill trail. Only then did Fraioch leave her perch, coming down the trunk head first. On the ground she sat tall to look, smell and listen before running to her den.

Mathair's cubs syne scrambled from their tunnel, two of them wedging in the entrance, bickering, and snapping at each other, until they forced their way clear. The third came out slowly, dragging her feet as though sick or in pain, and ignored the others when they started to play. She lay down near the tunnel entrance, with her chin on her outstretched forepaws, like a pining cat.

Presently Caileag's two cubs came lumbering along to make a foursome: the two families had found each other more than a week before. They played over half an acre of the slope, roughly and boisterously, without care or caution, yelping in excitement and yelping from play-bites. They chased up, down and across the slope, galloping in circles, loops and figures of eight; climbing on to rocks to become, fleetingly, kings of the castle; falling over boulders, crashing in the brushwood, bumping into trees and each other. No same number of piglets of their age could have stirred more tushkarue. Through it all Mathair's third cub lay in the same place, breathing heavily, watching without interest or urge to join them. And when the four, breaking off their play, bounded away to explore, she stayed behind, curled her nose to her flank and slept.

The exploring cubs fanned out, but not widely apart, keeping contact with the scent markers left by the sows. Sealgair, the tawny owl, flying to his nesting tree with a vole in his claws, startled them with a ringing war-whoop, but only for a moment. They stopped and listened, then padded on: they were no longer scared by his voice. They found little on their foray – a few worms, beetles, woodlice, slugs – and before long returned to the sett and went belowground. One of Caileag's cubs went nosing at the burrow where Fraioch was lying, and drew back in fright when she hissed at him, darted at him, and spat in his face.

While the badger cubs were underground Fraioch gave birth to eight blind, helpless kits, covered in silvery white gossamer hair. She licked them, and they squeaked in protest. When, later, she heard the badger romp again, she raised her head to listen, watching the entrance to her den, remembering Caileag's cub. But no cub came. Suddenly all was quiet outside; the cubs had gone away again. Fraioch drowsed, with her kits snugged into her belly, nosing for her nipples.

Four badger cubs wandered down to the burn, one hundred and fifty yards from home – not yet waywise but with the sows' scent markers to guide them out and signpost their way back: like seagoing salmon smolts registering scent impressions of their river and remembering them in reverse when returning upstream to spawn. The cubs might lose touch with each other, but none would become lost.

Mathair crossed the burn by stepping stones and called to her cubs – a staccato yap like a terrier's – and when they came to her she purred to them, and bocked up food for them, snapping at Caileag's twins to keep them away from her vomit. Then Caileag arrived and bocked up food for her own. Afterwards the cubs danced round their mothers, yelping their excitement. If Mathair was missing the third member of her family she betrayed no sign of it for, after setting scent on the pair, she left them, followed by Caileag, to resume her foraging. The cubs returned to the sett.

Two hours before dawn, with the wind breathing threat of rain, the cubs left the sett again to explore, and this time they travelled even farther afield, extending their frontier beyond the signs left by their mothers and setting scent of their own. They hearkened, without panic, to the *bough-bough* of a roebuck across the burn: they knew what it was. In time they would learn that dogs bark too. Within an hour they were back at the sett and Fraioch, suckling her kits, heard the yelps and thuds of them before they went to ground.

Bodach was at Drochaid Farm, prowling along the cornfield endrigg and the hedgerow, gobbling up slugs and scraping for earthworms. The ground was moist and worms were surfacing, but not enough of them for him to gorge on as he would have liked. Remembering the rabbit he had taken from a snare, he followed the hedgerow fence line, in the hope of finding another. But he found no rabbits because all the snares had been removed from the bottom wire. What he did find was new to him: the tongue of an Aberdeen Angus calf. It had been sliced off by a snare wire when he pulled back in terror after pushing it into the noose. Drummond saw the calf's bloodied mouth when he was looking over his beasts next morning, and it had been destroyed by a veterinary surgeon before the day was out, because it could neither graze nor suck.

After sniffing over the tongue Bodach tasted it. The taste was good so he ate it. In the past he had eaten kipper skins, herring heads and over-ripe fruit from the Drochaid Farm midden, and he had licked pig meal and poultry meal from outside feeding troughs; but this was the first time he had tasted tongue. With some excitement he nosed along the fence as though hoping to find another, not realising that calves' tongues in hedgebottoms are rare fauna indeed.

With his mind now set on home he slipped under the bottom wire of the fence and crossed the inbye pasture where five Aberdeen Angus cows now had four calves at foot. Four cows were grazing; the fifth was restless, running this way and that, or walking the fence line calling for her calf. She followed Bodach to the far fence, watched him slip through into the ride, then trotted back to the middle of the field *moo-ing* her plaint.

In the ride, halfway to the larch wood, Bodach found a rabbit burrow near the base of a split rowan. Wool mixed with earth scrapings at the entrance betrayed it as a nesting stop. The smell in it was rabbit, but he could also smell hedgehog. With sure instinct he found the spot on the ground directly above the nest and began to dig. While he was digging, with head down and nose full of earth smell, the hedgehog squeezed out quietly, and scurried almost tip-toeing away. She had rabbit fluff on her quills and three young in a nest under a stump at the Drochaid end of the ride.

Tough rowan roots impeded Bodach's digging and he had to bite them off to reach the nest of hay and wool. In it were five small rabbits, one of them half eaten by the hedgehog. He scooped them out, sneezed rabbit wool, and ate them where he stood – not biting and shearing with the side of his mouth but munching them whole. Now he was replete and wanting to lie up. Perhaps for that reason, or because of the pearling in the eastern sky, going home now became for him less urgent. He had other temporary dens where he could go to ground for a day, and he set off at a slow shuffle to the nearest of them.

The hole, five feet deep, with rock sides and bottom, was under a lichened scaur, yellow starred with tormentil, on the edge of the larch wood. There he could feel secure against anything except the wrong kind of dogs, in the right mood. With the daylight came two dogs, the right kind for him but in the wrong mood . . .

They were small, young and callow: halflin terriers of a sort. They were the new pets of a retired lady in the village, and had not till then been away from home on their own. All they knew about was chasing cats: yet there they were, suddenly, face to face with a great boar badger, yapping him awake and having no idea what to do about him.

Simon Fraser, out early after foxes, heard them before he saw them. Ordering down his own pair of hard-bitten, varminty terriers, he walked forward to a viewpoint, and there they were – ungaffered, sclaffing and ryving at a hole under the scaur, and by the yammering of one and the gurry-worries of the other they were excited about something yirdit out of their reach. One was a touzy West Highland white, with clayey purlies on her whiskers; the other was even smaller, and not easy to put a name to, but Simon guessed a dram of Cairn in a mixture of waters.

He went up to them, and spoke to them, but other than a twitch of stump tails and a mirthless grin, they had nothing to say, and went back to work. 'It'll be a rabbit they've got,' Simon thought to himself, misled by the way they were into the hole up to their necks and offering their faces to whatever. He grabbed and hoisted the West Highlander, and it was then he noticed the nick on her nose. That made him think of fox, which made the dogs' business his.

But what he saw when he kneed down and looked into the

hole was a candy-striped face in monochrome, Bodach's face – the biggest badger face he had ever seen. Knowing what a big badger could do to two small, inexperienced dogs he grabbed the Cairn mixture, oxtered the pair of them, and carried them aside, wondering how he was going to stop them from returning to the hole, or what he would do with them even if he could get the string from his pocket and tie them up.

He took the pair of them under his right arm and reached into his left pocket for binder twine to tie them with. The West Highlander struggled free and bolted back to the hole, barking and wagging her tail. The Cairn dram squirmed in his arms, and pawed his face, trying to break loose, but Simon managed to hold him and put a string on him, tight enough to hold him but not to choke him. Then he caught up the West Highlander again and tied her too. He walked them to the wood edge, tied them to a larch, and sat down to talk to them.

'If you chaps are ettlin to get your faces wasted you're sure gaun the richt way about it,' he told them in his characteristic amalgam of Gael's English and Scots. 'That chap in there's a professional and if he comes oot he'll decorate the baith of you for life and that could be short.' They wagged their tails and grinned at him.

Bodach would certainly have cut them up, perhaps mauled them seriously, if Simon had left them to taunt him. He had the *Bydand* up and he was not coming out that day, or any other day, for any two dogs, because his rock den was impregnable. No dog could dig to him, and none could get behind him. And the dog had yet to be born that could draw him.

Simon let the pair loose again, with the strings attached, hoping they would go away, but back to the hole they would be. He swore at them, profusely and profanely, and they skulked round him with their tails down; but always they would be back to the hole, drawn irresistibly by the badger magnetism. In the end he walked them to Drochaid Farm where he had left his Land Rover, calling up his own terriers to follow, but warning them to keep a distance, in case they took a notion to worry his captives.

The young constable at the Police Office was a keeper's son and an angler, and he was tying a fly when Simon arrived with the dogs.

'I found this pair of scallywags at a badger hole asking for trouble,' he told the policeman. 'Do you ken whose dogs they are?'

'I do that,' the policeman said. 'They belong to an old dear, a retired doctor they say, that's just taken over Riverside Cottage. She'll be worried about them, but grand pleased you've found them.'

'She'd be a damned sight worrieder if I'd left them where I found them,' Simon said.

'That'll be right,' the policeman agreed. 'Maybe you should've left them where they were and let them learn the hard way. It would've made them or broke them, whit!'

Simon said nothing. He took out his pipe and palmed over his breast pocket and side pockets looking for matches.

'Are you seeking fire?' the policeman asked.

'I am that,' Simon said.

The policeman handed him a box of matches.

Bodach returned to the sett at nightfall and found Mathair scratching her height against the trunk of a long-dead topless rowan, a claw-post he often used himself, and which had been used by many badgers before them. His topmost claw marks were the topmost of all and between them and the ground the rowan obelisk had an hour-glass figure: thus had their scratching worn and waisted it. Bodach reared against it and gouged with his foreclaws like a cat, grooving and furrowing it further. Mathair waited for him, touched noses with him, and they set their scent on each other. For some minutes afterwards she cast around as though searching for something; then she grunted to him and left.

Her ailing cub had died that afternoon and she had spent the past hour entombing it in a side pocket of the tunnel leading to Caileag's nesting chamber. She had dug the pocket to a depth of three feet, dragged the cub into it, drawn in or pushed back the soil, then padded it firmly with her forepads until the tomb was sealed. There the cub might lie for ever or a century, or be disinterred years later by other badgers digging other tunnels, when its bones would appear on one of the mounds built up like a line of fortifications along the frontage of the sett.

After Mathair left Bodach went belowground and found the place, and perhaps his nose told him what was buried there. He pushed along the tunnel to Caileag's nursery, came out by her exit, and took the uphill trail. There was no fresh scent of her all the way to the cut-over wood.

The yearling sow had not returned to the sett the previous morning; for reasons of her own she had gone to ground in new diggings beyond The Corrach near the boundary fence. There she met a two-years-old boar from across the river and paired with him, although she was not yet in breeding condition. Yearling sow badgers, like yearling bitch foxes, mate later than their elders. But whereas the cubs of yearling vixens are born that much later than the others, badger cubs are all born within the same short period; for badgers, like stoats, have a drawn-out pregnancy, with true development of their young beginning just before or after the year's shortest day, whatever the time of mating.

Chapter Five

Early on a morning of blue sky and larksong, mewing buzzards and croaking ravens, with peewits wavering in bat flight over the lower spurs and knowes, Coll MacDonald and Simon Fraser went to the hill to visit the eagles' eyrie. Blackface ewes with lambs were maggots moving on the shadowed flank of Ben Dearg: below them black and red cattle were grazing. With them the men had Coll's black Labrador retriever Sgian – a big-boned dog, deep-flewed, with wide skull, otter tail and chest with plenty of heart room. He was the steadiest dog on Dalnabreac and the best game finder.

The stalkers had spied the eyrie from half a mile away and seen that Fior-eun was sitting close; but they wanted to know what she was sitting on and the only way to find out was to visit her. They took great pride in their eagles, which bred success-fully every year.

It took them twenty minutes to reach the big scree of Ben Dearg – a wild jumble and sprawl of rocks and boulders spilling down for a thousand feet below the eyrie's ledge. It was a fearsome place, unchancy, the haunt of wildcat, fox and moun-tain badger; in olden times, when the Great Forest still stood, wolves had bred there. Across the scree was a shadowy trail, worn and darkened by the hooves of many generations of red deer.

The deer trail led aslant and up, levelling off below the eyrie. The men followed it, calling loudly to each other and rattling their sticks against rocks to warn Fior-eun of their coming: Coll never liked to take a nesting eagle by surprise. They were fifty yards from the eyrie, and below it, when Fior-eun came off, leaping into the air and banking steeply before gliding across the glen in rocking flight, her wingtips spread-fingered and upcurled.

The men climbed to the nest, which had a new frontage of woodrush, brought in by Iolair that morning. In it were two fat eaglets in white down. They were twelve days old and their crops were bulging. Beside them lay three plucked grouse, the haunch of a hare, and the intact body of a hoodie crow. Farther along the ledge, outside the nest, were two partly plucked rabbits and a rat smothered in flies. Sgian, seated below the rock, watching the men, sniffed up at the elusive, exciting smells.

'Nae shortage here,' Coll said to Simon.

'Indeed no!' Simon agreed. 'By here, this eaglets canny be bose!'

Fior-eun was wheeling five hundred feet above Ben Dearg, and Coll knew she was seeing them when they hurried away from the nest, following the deer trail, with Sgian at heel. After a quarter of a mile they turned downhill – running, jumping, skidding – and when they were far below the eyrie they veered left, heading back in the direction from which they had come. Fifteen minutes later they sat down on a flat-topped boulder and lit their pipes.

Coll held his stick at arm's length with its tip on the rock, unslung his telescope, and cradled it between his thumb and the ewe horn crook. He spied first their back trail and watched Fior-eun returning to her nest; then he swung the glass slowly, along the Slainte towards The Corrach. Soon he picked up three blackcocks on their lek his side of the river, and without taking his eye from the glass he said to Simon: 'I see three of thur silly chaps still lekking awa yet.' He watched them while two sheep with lambs walked across the lek, swung the glass away again, pin-pointed a kestrel hovering, then held it steady on a grey object across the river. He watched it closely, saw movement, and said to Simon:

'Put your glass down yonder, Simon, and see what can you see. Through the lek, then one o'clock. Something grey and it's moving.'

Simon lined up his glass and looked, his hand steady, his eye concentrating.

'Looked like a bit rock at first, till it moved,' he said. 'Not a lamb surely; it's not white enough. But I'm not seeing all of it. A ewe maybe?'

'Or maybe a badger?' Coll was thinking aloud.

Simon looked again. 'You could be right at that. If it is, it's in a trap.'

'Or in a snare,' said Coll. 'Let's to the Piper's Cairn Simon. We'll get a better look from there.'

At the Piper's Cairn they sat down, wedged their sticks, and cradled their telescopes. Sgian nosed the end of Coll's glass and he had to wipe it clear. 'Keep your tongue to yoursel, man,' he chided the dog. The men picked the object up almost at once. It was bigger to the eye now, but there was less of it showing. Then it moved and they were looking at the unmistakable striped face of a badger. The beast was in a fox snare.

'Well, that's it then,' Coll said. 'But I thocht there was supposed to be nae badgers left on that side?'

'That's the way the mannie tells it, accordin tae the chaps that ken him,' Simon agreed, slapping his glass shut. 'It's the auld bit about the only good badger bein a sporran.'

'That bit I ken, Simon. Where he cam fae they called him the *Brochan*, so I'm told.'

'The what?'

Coll laughed quietly, without mirth. 'It's Gaelic, Simon. Gaelic for a badger hunter – ane that kills badgers for sporrans. Onyway he'll likely be along syne to chap the beast on the head.'

'Now that,' said Simon, 'I wouldn't bet on. They say he's never in a hurry lookin his traps. Remember last spring, no long after he cam here, yon boy scout chaps comin on a fox and it had been stripped clean by the hoodies?'

'Right then. We'd best gang hame and call him on the phone.'

'I could nick across and pit the beast oot o its misery,' Simon offered.

'No! That's when the mannie would be sure to turn up, and by heck you'd get your shirt tail set on fire, for sure. We'll phone him.'

They hurried home and telephoned, but there was no answer. They tried several times, at half hour intervals, but there was still no answer. Coll was thinking of driving the eight miles to the keeper's house when there was a knock on the door. Sgian did not bark for he knew who the caller was. It was the shepherd, with something bulky stuffed in his bag, wrapped in his yellow oilskin cape.

'Come in, Pharic,' Coll greeted him. 'We're in a bit of a stramash here wondering how tae let the mannie on the ither side ken he's got a badger in a snare, still alive.'

'By here,' Pharic said, stroking Sgian and pushing his nose away from the bag, 'you chaps must be needing your een tested, whatever! I was up in the wee corrie and got you in the glass when you were spying from the Piper's Cairn. When I cam down, guess what I found below the cairn?'

Coll and Simon stared at him. 'What?'

'This!' Pharic said, unslinging the bag and laying his burden on the floor. Sgian sniffed at the package, wagging his stern furiously and whimpering with excitement.

'Come on now, Pharic,' Simon laughed. 'What's the mystery? What's in there?' Coll looked at the shepherd, wondering, for Pharic had the droll bit in him and could be a master of ellipsis when it suited him.

'A badger,' he announced. 'Alive but just. That sair snared the wire's buried in its neck. I found it stacherin aboot below the cairn an hour or so after you chaps left.'

54

'But there's nae snares on Dalnabreac,' Coll reminded him.

'Quite so,' Pharic agreed, 'but there's this one now, and on Dalnabreac it was, complete with badger whatever.'

'But what about the one we were looking at?' Simon asked. 'The one on the ither side?'

Pharic thought for a moment, rubbing his chin, and said: 'All I saw there was through the glass, and you chaps should take a look at that corner some time. It's a slughterhouse, with an owl hanging flapping from a pole trap and the place littered aboot wi dead buzzards, owls and whatever. But I saw no badger when I spied it.'

'But you canna see the pole trap from the corrie or The Piper's,' Coll objected.

'From where I was you could,' Pharic replied.

'It must be the same badger,' Coll insisted.

'Well now, it could be, I suppose,' Pharic admitted. 'Maybe it crossed the Slainte, eh?'

'Cross the Slainte, my auntie Kate!' Simon exploded with a mocking laugh.

'If it's in the state you say, Pharic, it would hae drowned trying to cross the river,' said Coll.

'I didn't say it crossed the river,' Pharic said. 'Maybe it did and maybe it didn't. But The Piper's was where it was.'

'I'll tak a bet,' Simon said, 'that if I was tae gang back up there this minute, there'd be a badger on the ither side, in a snare.'

'I doubt it, Simon,' Coll said to him, looking quizzically at Pharic. 'Likely the mannie'll hae been up there by this time and taken it awa.'

'Not likely, if you ask me,' said Pharic. 'Hae ye forgotten what day this is? It's Sunday, the Sabbath, ken? The mannie'll be at the kirk, him bein an elder and all, and that's twelve miles away. Then it'll be the bar on the quiet likely after that for a whiley. I'm thinking he winna be up there the day.'

'Right then,' said Coll, 'let's first hae a look at your badger, then you'll have the dram after that yourself, Pharic, surely?'

'Well, I've been kent tae refuse but I'm damned if I can mind

55

when was the last time. Where'll we tak the beast?'

'Into the larder. There's the big table there we can lay it on. You chaps gang in while I get a muzzle and a sack needle. And Pharic! Have you tied the beast's legs?'

'Only the hind ones. I kept away from the business end.'

Pharic put his bag on the table and gently eased out the contents. Coll had put on horsehide gauntlets, but when he peeled back the oilskin there was no snake-dart of head or snap of jaws. Although the beast was exhausted and weak, its eyes closed and its breathing shallow, Simon put the muzzle on it just in case. Coll turned the body on to its side, exposing the point where the wire disappeared into the neck: the noose was deeply embedded and out of sight.

'It's a sow,' Pharic observed, more to himself than the others. 'But not being sooked.' He ran his experienced fingers over her midriff and belly. She was the yearling from Bodach's sett.

Pharic and Simon held her down firmly while Coll set to work with the sack needle, probing for the noose close to where the wire entered her neck hoping, if he found it, to pull the slack through the eyelet. But the wire was knotted and locked there, and would not be pulled. After further probing he managed to get the curved needle under the noose, and when he could see it he asked Simon for cutters:

'The wee ones, Simon, with the fine neb. They're in the drawer beside you there.'

With hands as steady and gentle as a surgeon's he cut the noose, took hold of the free wire, and unwound the snare. The badger stirred then and opened her eyes, but there was no fight in her. She sighed and began to breathe more easily. When she flicked out her tongue Coll fetched some milk, dipped a wad of cotton wool into it, and squeezed some of it through her teeth. She licked it in. He squeezed in more, and she licked again.

'She might make it yet,' said Pharic.

'She might at that,' Coll said to him, 'but if this Suez canal round her neck goes septic, I wouldn't give a snowball's chance for her. Simon! Would you phone the Vet at his house? Good! And now, Pharic! You'll hae that dram?'

56

They laid her back on the table when the Veterinary Surgeon arrived. After his examination of her he said to Coll: 'The throat needs stitching. The rest should mend by itself. But she'll have bother swallowing for a while.' While Coll spanned her jaws, the Vet cut the hair along both sides of her throat wound, dusted it with white powder, then put four strong stitches in it. He dusted right round her neck, then gave her an injection. 'Try that and see how you get on,' he said. 'Any problems – don't hesitate to call me.'

They wrapped her in an old blanket and carried her out to a single kennel away from the terriers; it had a concrete floor and was enclosed by steel railing. Simon put in a bale of clean oat straw, while Coll brought a dish with milk and two raw eggs; if she could not chew or swallow, he thought, she might be able to drink.

'She won't dig her way out of there, anyway,' he said.

'That's for sure,' Simon agreed. 'The only thing she's likely tae be digging is her grave!'

'I think she has a chance, Simon,' said Pharic. 'Maybe she'll make it, maybe not, but I think maybe!'

Coll closed and bolted the kennel door. 'I think we'll leave her now till tomorrow. There's nothing more we can do. You'll have another dram before you go, Pharic?'

'Och, yes, thank ye. I have a terrible taste of disinfectant in my mouth.'

Next morning Coll found the milk and eggs untouched, and gave the dish to Sgian. That evening he put down fresh milk and eggs, and in the morning the dish was empty. The badger was balled up in the straw, with her face between her forepaws, and not moving; but she had food taken, as Coll told it later, and he was satisfied. After that he gave her oatmeal gruel, with a lot of milk and a little honey. Ten days later she was eating rabbit, with the bones removed, in addition to milk and soaked hound meal. At the end of three weeks she was eating whole rabbit with anything else he gave her, and *woofing* at him if he approached her too closely. And he knew it was time for her to go.

He had made up his mind to put her in the Breac sett, but a mile was the closest he could get to it in the Land Rover. That mile was the problem. He guessed that she would not be carried there, stuffed in the shepherd's bag, as she had been carried in: she was a gey brock again, fit and strong, and likely she would fight and bite.

'What'll you take her in?' asked Pharic. 'A blanket?'

Coll thought for a moment. 'No. In the toolbox. It's heavy, I ken, but it's got handles and Simon and I should manage.'

'I'll lend a hand if you like. Is it tomorrow night you're going?'

'No. First thing in the morning. That'll give her the day to settle and sort herself out.'

'Make it early then. I'm for the hill at six. But, look you, are you not for marking her to ken her again?'

'I doubt we'll be seeing her again, Pharic . . . But supposing we did . . . and she was marked . . . But how?'

'I'll keel her for you,' Pharic grinned. 'I ken she's a sow but she'll nae mind looking like a yowe for a whiley.'

Pharic keeled her in bright blue, dabbing a broad band along her back, from behind her neck wound to the root of her scut. Then he stood back, like an artist appraising his work. 'How's that?'

'What do we call her, then?' Simon asked. ' "Rangers lass?" '

'Hell, no!' Pharic said. ' "Celtic girl" would be more in keeping, except the colour's wrong. What about "Keely"?'

And thus they named the Breac yearling, now sixteen months old. They carried her to the sett and chose a used tunnel between Mathair and Caileag to put her in, not knowing it had been her own or that she was of the Breac clan. A jay, perched on a grape cluster of marble galls and screened by young leafage, watched them while they spilled her from the toolbox then flew *squeching* away. Keely trundled belowground without hesitation, knowing where she was: the men backed away to watch and she did not come out again. Pharic called his two collies to heel and left for the hill. Half an hour later, with still no sign of Keely surfacing, Coll and Simon felt sure she would stay where she was and set off on their back trail to the Land Rover. They had already decided to return to the sett in the evening to see if she was still there.

Half an hour before sunset Sealgair, the tawny owl, saw two men crossing the burn and stood tall to stare at them. Bodach, lying half awake at the entrance to his tunnel, had no knowledge of them: they were downwind, stalking cat-footed into the oaks, and their movements were beyond his range of vision. But Fraioch, the bitch stoat, winded them and saw them, and bounded to her den, leaving behind the young rabbit she had been hefting and half-dragging home to her kits. She would retrieve it later.

The men climbed into the stag-headed oak from which Coll had first viewed the badgers and seated themselves in crotches. They snipped off leafy twigs to give them a clearer view of the sett. Farther up the slope they could hear the wheezing of owlets; Sealgair's mate and her flying owlets were now on the badgers' side of the Breac.

Bodach heaved out on to his mound and the men could see the white face of him in the sun-dappled shadows; they could not see the fat toad crab-walking past within a paw stroke of his nose. A pied woodpecker dipped from an oak, down across the burn and up into the pines on the other side. Bodach sat up, like a dog begging, combing his belly and chest with his foreclaws, scratching upwards to his throat. Although both men had their eyes fixed on him Coll saw something else and nudged Simon to look down and to the right: a black-and-white face was framed in the hole where they had put Keely.

Left and right the striped arrow-face swivelled, sniffing the threshold earth, nostrils gathering scents, ears wavelengthed for any sound, eyes focusing but incapable of seeing form without movement. The face thrust out, followed by shoulders, then withdrew, thrust out and sniffed again. The men watched. The badger came right out on to the mound and they could see the dark broad band along its back. It was Keely.

She winded Bodach and padded towards him; he saw her and came forward to meet her. She tried to climb over him but he drew back as though suspicious of her. She sat down and set her scent on the ground, and Bodach sniffed the spot. Mathair appeared, and joined him, and they sniffed Keely's scent together. Caileag now came shambling along the slope, and presently the men were watching four badgers jostling, grappling and falling over each other. Then . . .

Thud!

'Jesus Christ!' exclaimed Simon in a whisper when he felt the blow on his right ear. Instinctively his hand went to it, and he knew it was bleeding. Realising at once that the badgers had disappeared he reached without stealth for his handkerchief, folded it, and padded it on the ear.

'It's the bliddy owl!' Coll said in a low voice, surprised more than angry, and almost as he said it the bird attacked again, unseen and noiselessly, and struck him between the shoulders. Then they heard her savage war-whoop, above and behind them, and pulled up their collars, keeping their faces down chin to chest. The owl made a third swoop, and hit Coll hard on the back of the head. That was her last, and she flew away, the *wee-wicking* of her fading in the oakwood.

'What the hell does she want to go clouting us for?' Coll said half aloud. 'Her young ones are flying about and nowhere near the nest.'

'I ken what I would like to do with the bitch,' Simon told him, looking at the blood on his white handkerchief, then putting it back on his ear and holding it there. 'And she's frightened awa the badgers.'

'Gave them a start, maybe,' Coll whispered. 'The main thing is they don't ken we're here. So we'll hang on a wee yet. Badgers dinna fleg that easy.'

The afterglow was fading when four badgers emerged from one tunnel, treading on each other's scuts, and the men realised at once that Keely was not among them. The four were cubs and they quickly wandered off downhill. Then Keely appeared, followed by Mathair and Caileag, and this time there was no greeting or ritual scenting of each other: they all went downhill on the trail taken by the cubs. Minutes passed before Bodach came out and rushed uphill, without testing the wind or taking time to scratch himself.

'That was a fair hantle of badgers,' Simon remarked. 'I wonder if . . .'

'Look down there, Simon!' Coll interrupted him. Simon looked, and what they saw was Fraioch, homing with her rabbit, which had been missed by eight badgers because it was lying downwind and they had not gone that way. They watched Fraioch pulling it, pushing it, hefting it, upending it, wraxing it towards her den, until she disappeared in the uphill gloom. Then they climbed down from their perches.

By the time they reached home Simon's ear was swollen and painful, like the classical cauliflower of the fighting trade. The doctor examined it, taped a pad on it, and gave him an anti-tetanus injection, remarking vaguely that such dangerous birds should not be encouraged. Simon did not say he had been watching badgers at the time. Coll went to bed early, was up again at two o'clock in the morning, and off to the badger sett within fifteen minutes. He wanted to see if Keely came back.

This time he approached the big oak tree from above, because seven badgers had gone downhill the night before and he did not want to leave his fresh scent on the slope below in case they came back the same way. That would make them uneasy and suspicious. It was five minutes to three o'clock when he took his seat in the tree. A fresh wind was stirring the leaves, like pebbles stirred by a tide.

Sealgair flew from across the burn and Coll watched him pitch in a wide-branched alder on the flat. After that he could make out only the movement of him among the leafage, as he shuffled, spread a wing, or bowed on his perch. Four times, withershins, frog-croaking and chirping, a woodcock flew round the clearway on his morning circuit. A robin flicked on to a branch beside Coll, peered at him with its bright eyes, then flew down to peck in the ground litter. Coll looked at his watch. The time was 3.10.

Syne he saw a white arrowhead weaving uphill, dabbing at the dark, and again he was reminded of a yoked horse nodding. The badger, not hurrying but not loitering, walked on to the mound farthest away, bounded from it to the next, and the next, until it was on the one almost directly below him. It was Keely. She sat up with her back to him, finger-clawed herself for a minute or so, dived into her tunnel, turned about, and crouched at the entrance, facing out. The white of her face was soiled, and she had dried earth crusted on her nose: she had been rooting late on in the night.

Mathair and Caileag arrived on each other's heels and went to ground at once. The light was coming up before Bodach arrived at a spring-footed trot, with his belly full of earthworms and rabbit and one thought in his head: he ran to Keely purring. She came out and greeted him, then went bounding along the slope like the giant weasel she was, with Bodach porpoising after her. Down to the burn they went, and back again, and Coll could hear the thuds of their feet. At last they sat down under the oak, with Keely setting her scent on Bodach's rump. When he tried to groom her throat with his front teeth she drew back from him: it was still her sensitive spot.

Woodpigeons flapped from the oaks with slap and clatter of wings; a cock pheasant crowed; across the Breac a woodpecker started drumming. Keely broke away from Bodach and went to ground. Bodach dawdled to his own entrance, stood for a moment on the mound, then disappeared from view. But he was still there, crouched, facing out, waiting for the early morning sun.

Coll was puzzled by the absence of the cubs, so he waited on until sunrise. He had no way of knowing that they were lying up on the far side of The Corrach, in the same diggings used by Keely when she first left home. Nor did he realise when he left by the way he had come that Bodach was still lying aboveground, as unaware of the man's presence as the man was of his.

Chapter Six

Fraioch's eight kits – five dogs and three bitches – were playing up, down and round about Bodach's scratching post when he came in from Drochaid on a stainless steel windless morning, with his belly full of earthworms, his legs sleeked with dew and dandruffed with hayseed fernitickles. Poor sighted, even in the flat half-light of a sunless sunrise, and because there was no wind, he was almost at his scratching post before his nose could own their scent or his eyes see the movements of them. But they could see the massive, white-fronted bulk of him, plodding along the slope, while he was yet many paces away, and were in action before he found them with his nose.

Seven of them, that is!

The three at the bottom of the post bounded away towards their den; the four on the climb-down or climb-up leaped to the ground and followed them. That left one on top – a strong dog kit as big as Fraioch. Bodach reared, stretched his length, and clawed the post: on top the dog kit stood four-legged tall and peered down at him with dark, shining eyes. His escape route was blocked and he knew it.

There are those who think that badgers are too ponderous and flat-footed to climb trees, and certainly they are not as nimble as the fox, or to be compared with the stoat, or even the polecat. But climb they can, and sometimes do.

Bodach started to climb, hugging the trunk, gripping fast with foreclaws and hind, heaving himself up like a bear, or a linesman on a telephone pole. He was four feet from the ground when the stoat kit came down – hissing, head first and at speed. He was sure-footed, agile, a will-o-the-wisp, and here indeed was the ponderous badger, the cumbersome bear-weasel, outclassed in everything except weight and weaponry, and these of no avail. The stoat kit leaped over his head, footed him fleetingly on the rump, then was on the ground and away. And all Bodach knew of him was a glimpse of a small shape coming at his face and the light-footed touch on his rump.

A cuckoo flew into a nearby oak tree, bowed with wings half open and long tail in the air, and called: *Cu-coo; cu-coo-coo: a-wiss-a-wiss*. The bird watched as Bodach climbed down backwards and dropped the last three feet, with his claws furrowing the post. On the ground he shook himself, then dawdled to the mound in front of his tunnel, turned about, and bellied down to lick his forepaws.

Four tits, a redstart and a blackbird alighted near the cuckoo, scolded what they had to say, and the hawk-like bird flew away. The small birds did not pursue. Bodach heard them without listening: their small talk had no meaning for him. But when a hoodie crow pitched on the rowan obelisk, and there began to caw harshly and stab between his feet, he became alert. Crow talk was talk he listened to.

Mathair arrived on the uphill trail and he recognised her tread; when she came on to the mound he recognised her scent. She touched noses with him and went belowground, and he resumed his paw licking. But before long – while the crow still stood on the post picking off flinders of dead bark and tossing them to the ground – she was out again, backing on to the mound with a bundle of old bedding clasped to her chest. She backed on to Bodach before he moved out of her way. When she

64

went below again he crab-walked to another mound along the frontage. It was partly mossed over and the entrance to the tunnel behind it was filled with dead leaves.

The hoodie passed guttural comment on his move, and he was hardly bellied down when a robin whirred in and alighted close to his face. It tilted its head and looked at him with bright, elderberry eyes: pot-bellied but upstanding, a potato on match sticks. Bodach blinked and sniffed. The robin bowed and pecked speculatively in a patch of green velvet. Bodach yawned. A rabbit screamed. The robin whirred away.

Bodach sat up and hearkened. He knew the cry. From his own mouth he had heard it when he snatched a rabbit in his jaws. Silence, lasting minutes, followed the scream. The hoodie lifted from the post and flew away in its direction; perhaps he recognised the sound too and was hoping to profit from it, being an opportunist predator on many things and a scavenger of anything. Bodach listened on.

More minutes passed. Then he heard a muted, croodling chain link of sound that was neither dove nor blackcock: a sound, not menacing, that might have been uttered by a bird. But no bird had uttered it. It was Fraioch's summons to her kits, and syne all eight were bounding across Bodach's front – slim-bodied, sinuous, sinewy, with rumps arched and white flanks flashing: five ahead in line abreast and three abreast following, croodling in reply. In a moment they were beyond his vision, and out of his nose because there was no wind. But they were not far away.

Fraioch had tracked the rabbit, ignoring all others, and killed it by a bite on the neck where it was now lying, close to the outermost entrance to the sett, long disused by the badgers. It was more than twice her weight so she could not move it, but she wanted it under cover, especially with a hoodie waiting on. Her kits leaped on it with great excitement, tugging at the fud, burying their faces in the fur, climbing all over it and getting in each other's way. They had no idea what she wanted to do with it.

They licked and bit at the bloody patch on its neck, and

65

hiss-snarled at each other in mock savagery. Fraioch gripped it by a foreleg and tugged. Three kits joined her, fastening their teeth in ear, nose and throat; one climbed on the body and bit fur; four took hold near the fud and pulled the other way. In the end, with six pulling against three, and one watching, she had the rabbit under cover, and all of them began to eat.

Unlike the crow, Bodach had not been tempted to go seeking after a rabbit killed by a stoat. Instead he helped Mathair in bringing out bedding and spreading it on the mound. Farther along Keely was also dragging out bedding, and when he visited Caileag he found her doing the same. They worked on until long after normal badger bed-time, then all went below ground for the rest of the day.

About the middle of the morning, when big-bellied clouds like sagging cobwebs were smothering the crown of Ben Dearg and threatening rain, Fraioch's kits left their den again to play, running in line ahead to the oak tree from which Coll and Simon had viewed their mother. Against its calloused trunk they played an intricate and stamina testing game of pairs. They spaced themselves round it, as though choosing the four points of the compass. The pairs leaped their height, half rolled as their forepaws touched the trunk, then curved away, thrusting with their hindpads, back to the ground. Their leaps, turn-aways and landings were synchronised, and they performed perfect figures of eight without collisions.

This testing game they played for about three minutes then, as though at a prearranged signal, they broke off and bounded in single file to a windfall, along which they began to play follow my leader. During this game they crooned and chittered, happy sounds not often heard by human ear. They were like dancers performing a sequence of figures, for next they all leaped from the windfall and continued their game on the ground: sitting up, crouching, standing tall, darting, circling and somersaulting – curduddich and rigadoon, with mouth music, at bewildering speed. Now and again a pair would grapple and roll over in embrace, wriggling and cavorting like cut earthworms.

Rain came to stop their game and they all bounded back to

their den. Soon it was a steady downpour. Hour after hour it sheeted down. The Breac became a mill race of glassy water, covering the badgers' stepping stones and flooding the flats of butterbur and water avens, sallow and speedwell. At darkening the sky cleared and the rain died away. Sealgair detached himself from the trunk of his roosting tree, against which he had been standing tall like a roll of withered bark, side-stepped along his perch and shook water from his plumage. He clicked his beak and said *wee-wick*; but did not hoot.

The stoat kits came out again, and were drenched in their wild scamper into the ferns and grass tussocks. This time Fraioch was with them. They gathered to her croon-call and she led them away uphill on the badger trackway, eight following her in line like links in a chain. Their games had developed muscle and poise, speed and accuracy of pounce; now they were ready to learn the art of hunting for themselves.

When Bodach and Mathair appeared the trees were still dripping and the darkening restless with the sound of running water. They were soon joined by Caileag and Keely, and for a while they played a subdued game of chasing each other under the oaks, up and down the slope, and through ferns and brambles, soaking their outer fur and leaving clawed sclaffs on the glidders. Presently they returned to their tunnels and pulled out more old bedding. Caileag *woofed*, startled, when Sealgair swooped suddenly and snatched a woodmouse behind her back.

After dark they left for Drochaid to hunt; this would be a night for earthworms and slugs. While the sows dispersed to pastures, hedgerows and the cornfield edge Bodach wandered away to the hayfield where cutting had begun. He nosed along the sodden rows of swathes, from corner to corner of the field, and round it, catching two voles besides slugs, beetles and earthworms. Before daybreak he was back at the sett, followed soon by Mathair, whose face was earth stained: she had been rooting for chafer grubs. Caileag and Keely did not return.

For most of the day Bodach lay at the entrance to his tunnel, dozing and basking in a hot sun that brought out the flies. Jays were roistering in the oaks; blue tits were churring, carrying caterpillars to fledged young in the branches. He ignored them, hearing without listening. Then he heard a low clucking call from downhill, and that interested his ears and made him lift his head.

A hen capercaillie, in barred and chequered plumage with rufous breast, was walking past his scratching post, followed by five fat chicks fluttering and flighting and dabbing at flies. When she saw the badger's face she ran, head down, shrinking to half her size, with her brood flutter-flying after her. She had nested near the top of the slope, under bramble tendrils beside an old pine stump, less than twelve feet above the badgers' well trodden trail. Bodach yawned, settled down again, and dozed.

At nightfall he left with Mathair on the downhill trail to the Breac. Although the water was still glissading over their stepping stones they splashed across, kinaesthetically waywise, going where they wanted to go without looking where they were going. On the other side they shook themselves, but little water sprayed from their coats. Although their legs were sleeked with water up to their hocks and halfway to their elbows, their belly fur was almost dry.

On their way to The Corrach they came across the scents of Caileag and Keely on the trail, and marked the spot with their own. A hundred yards from the wood they turned off on a right fork, along a year-old runway not yet padded flat, which led to new diggings, two holes with low mounds in front, under the roots of a century old ash. Keely had denned here before she met the Ardcreag boar, and crossed the river with him to be caught in Colin Campbell's fox snare. Mathair's cubs were now using it, but they were not at home. Bodach and Mathair set scent outside it, and trotted back to the main trail which they followed into The Corrach.

From the wood edge to The Corrach sett it was a hidden runway, a narrow lane through ground cover of heather, blaeberries, scrub birch and ferns, roofed over at intervals with straggles of rowan and hazel. The sett was empty, but the scent in it was of Caileag and Keely. Bodach entered and sniffed over the bedding, while Mathair set her scent outside: then the pair

68

followed the trail to the Breac, and crossed by a sagging footbridge of larch planks, bleached and lichened with age and with tormentil growing in the cracks. On the other side was a vast area of moor grass stretching to The Piper's Cairn, and beyond it heather moor reaching up to the east flank of Ben Dearg.

Long eared owls, two adults and their young, were hunting the grassland for voles, which that year had reached a peak of numbers. A fox was hunting there too, leaping and pouncing in true fox style, clicking teeth and swallowing: he had seven voles in his belly and his mind set on catching more. The badgers ignored the fox and plodded on to the Piper's Cairn where they met Caileag's well grown, self reliant cubs, also hunting voles. The cubs ran to them, greeting them with muted grunts and yelps, and after the four had scented each other they all went vole harvesting. The harvest was bounteous and everything, furred or feathered, that ate voles was hunting them, by night or by day.

With their bellies full of voles the old badgers left the grassland and set out purposefully for the big scree of Ben Dearg, where they had an outlying den a thousand feet below the eagles' eyrie – a mile and a half by crow flight from the Breac sett and more than three by the way they had come.

The den at the bottom of the scree was at the limit of the Breac clan's territory, and beyond it they did not go; scent markers and latrines loosely defined its frontier.

To anyone familiar only with badgers of the fat lowlands it would not have seemed a sett at all, for there were no earth-works like fortifications to betray it. It was a deep, natural tunnel under the rocks, which radiated off into other lesser or greater tunnels, which in turn branched into yet other passages and openings: a hidden maze of tortuous highways, byways and dead ends where a hunting terrier could be lost for hours without meeting up with its fox.

The sun's rim was gilding the peak of Ben Dearg, and seven

ravens were already high, circling and wheeling against the blue, when Bodach and Mathair arrived at the sett. They knew none of their own clan would be there and were expecting, if they were expecting anything at all, no more than a fox squatter or perhaps a visiting badger from beyond the frontier. Instead they were greeted by an explosive hiss, and a *pfuff-pfuff*, followed by the sing-song, wailing pibroch of a wildcat fuming.

She came at them legged-up tall, with ringed tail bottle-brushed, ears flat and teeth bared; and a bristling she-devil she was, beautiful in her indomitable cattiness, prepared to face two badgers because she had three kittens behind her in one of their beds. The kittens were strong and active, well grown at ten weeks old. They grimaced and spat, and wailed their own kitten pibroch, copying their mother. The badgers backed off, not because they were afraid but because they needed time to decide what they were going to do about her.

Outside, Bodach sat down and scratched himself, while Mathair looked at the cat, wrinkling her nose at the taint. The wildcat came to the entrance, with back arched and bristling: and what a magnificent beast she was to be sure – with the glowering green moon eyes of her, and the girning grandeur of her, and the armed forepaw raised, and the sharp teeth of her showing, and the ears of her flattened round the curve of her skull. And for sure, too, there was that in her enough to make a grown man tremble; but what was her weaponry of tooth and claw against two big badgers, one of them the mightiest boar on Dalnabreac?

But her weaponry was not put to the test. Although she was hottring with cat venom at the badgers' intrusion, and prepared to fight in defence of her kittens, she had not yet reached the point of suicidal recklessness. So when Bodach thrust into the sett, with his head down and his chin tucked into his chest, the massive frontage of him daunted her, and she gave way yard by yard. Her kittens backed away behind her. She could have leaped on to his back – there was enough room – but her claws would have made little impression on his wiry back thatch. There was no way she could safely grapple with him to bring her

70

hindclaws into action, and no way they could have reached his underside whatever. In a grapple she might have had his eyes; but he would have had her life.

So she retreated, slowly and reluctantly, snarling and spitting and exploding in Bodach's face, dabbing at him with an armed forepaw, but she might as well have tried to stop a flash flood on the Breac. To the monstrous, muscular bulk of him she had no answer except her rage and her menacing pibroch. And Bodach was not impressed. Nor, to be sure again, was he wishing for a fight at all, for the *broc* is not a fighting person; he is a pacifist rather, mindful of his other cheek, and a great one for the neutrality and the peace conference. But what a terrible, ferocious, bone-breaking surgeon he can be when brought to the brulzie.

All the badgers wanted was their sleeping quarters, and with the wildcat out of the way they reclaimed their old beds, which were stale sure enough, but dry and not fouled. For Bodach and Mathair the turavee was over. And herself, the cat, was not inconvenienced either, for she took her kittens into another gallery, not far from the badgers, and bedded them in a dry hollow with its own exits. To them she was just another squatter, and they treated her as such, which meant they had no interest in her so long as she kept out of their way.

At mid morning an avalanche of mist swept down and the glen became a whiteout silence; then the rain came in a steady drizzle that lasted all day and far into the night. Four times in the night the badgers looked out and withdrew again; they still had vole comfort in their bellies and no mind for a soaking. The wildcat ventured on a brief foray, but caught nothing and returned to her kittens.

Before dawn the rain stopped and the sky cleared except for scattered wisps of cloud like lamb's fleece and a ringlet of white below the peak of Ben Dearg. Iolair and Fior-eun, with two young flying, were up before the sun, soaring and gliding, a thousand feet above the cloud ringlet. Seven ravens – Pruk, Borb and their family – were flapping and hopping about the eyrie, tugging at sticks to uncover old bones and skins, and

71

tossing them aside, passing time rather than hunting for leavings. The eaglets had been on the wing for a week and would not be returning.

Bodach was lying at the entrance to the tunnel, waiting for the sun and half asleep, but his ears brought him awake when they heard the near bleating of a lamb. Three ewes with lambs, out-rangers from Pharic's hirsel, were straggling towards the scree, the ewes walking in file, the lambs frolicking behind, light-footed after shedding the rain water from their fleeces.

The afternoon was warm, with a light wind from the southeast, and in the evening the badgers came out early. The sun was westering in plaid of flame with fiery banners streaming, and a honey-coloured moon was riding high. Mathair left Bodach and went her own way along the hillside, while he padded aslant and down till he reached The Spoot – a narrow burn that was a gusher when snow-fed and a trickle in dry summers. Tonight it was a wee torrent, rain-fed, and revelling in its head of water.

Bodach followed it down to where it yammered white-crested between high rocky banks. On one side birches grew from the water's edge to halfway up the terraced bank; the other face was draped with woodrush and ferns. From a cleft in one of the waterside birches a yearling red deer hind was hanging by the neck, dead. Stampeding with her group from a mock assault by Iolair she had leaped into the birch top, crashed through the branches, and caught her neck in the cleft as she fell, to die by strangulation. The branch was bent down by her weight, split but not broken.

Her hindfeet were touching the ground. Bodach sniffed her legs, then reared against the body, which swayed away from him. He was reaching with his teeth for a leg grip when Mathair arrived. They took hold together, each with a leg, and their weight, helped by their strength, brought the body lower, and the split in the branch lengthened. They pulled with all their strength; the split branch ripped away and the body slumped to the ground.

With their forepaws on the inside of the hind's thighs, they began to bite into her groin, ripping skin and exposing the entrails. They ate little of the entrails, working instead on the fleshy thighs; tugging, chewing and swallowing, and bloodying the white of their faces. Within half an hour they had gorged themselves. They drank from the burn, plunged their faces in the water, which washed off some of the blood, then set off for home. With the night hardly begun, and the moon still flushed from the afterglow, they were ready to go to bed.

Later in the night, while they were asleep, the wildcat winded the carcass and led her kittens to their first meal of venison. Nothing came to disturb them and they ate their fill – the big cat shearing flesh in silence, the kittens wailing their sing-song of ownership. Before she led them away, she tore off a sliver of thigh muscle, which she carried back to her den. All four were blood-whiskered and would be a long time cleaning.

Not long after they had gone a dog fox found the body and bellied down beside it to eat. Half a mile away his vixen had four well grown cubs hidden in a stand of tall bracken where they could move unseen by day: she had brought them a long way from her old den, which she left after discovering man-smell on her doorstep. Now she was a lost fox being looked for. She had brought five cubs to the bracken kennel, but Fior-eun had lifted one and carried it to the eyrie, where Pharic found it and tailed it. At the office he was paid ten shillings bounty for the tail.

The dog fox knew his vixen would not be coming his way that night; she was vole-hunting with the cubs in another direction. Yet the urge was on him to carry something home. He was a big fox, and powerful, with a strong will and good teeth. But what could he do with a freshly dead hind? Cut a leg? Not that, surely, or any bulk of meat. About what he did there is no question. He scraped at the entrails; he burst the paunch and dragged it out, spilling its green mash on the ground; then he bored into the belly cavity, and bit and pulled, and when he pulled out, red-faced with blood, he had the liver in his jaws. And with it he trotted away.

Bodach and Mathair were awake before daylight. Although not hungry they were drawn to go back to the venison, which has a fascination for every flesh eater on the hill, even down to weasels and shrews. The sky was clear, and the light coming up, so they made haste to The Spoot at a swinging trot, not ettling to be caught in the full glare of the morning sun.

And there – as they say in the classic understatement of the Gael – was a sight for eyes to see.

Seven ravens were at the carcass: three between the hindlegs and four on the flank stabbing through the ribs with their pick-axe beaks. On top of the opposite bank two eagles were standing – Fior-eun on one leg, looking about her, and Iolair with his head skewed and glaring at them. Not far away, on a rock as big as a shieling, were their two eaglets, asleep with beaks tucked into shoulders.

Iolair was impatient, but Fior-eun was prepared to wait until the ravens flew away. She had no wish to stir up the wrath of seven of them, for the black birds of Odin can be an eagle's nightmare. The badgers had no such fears; indeed, being mainly beasts of the night, unfamiliar with the daylight scene, they knew little about ravens. So they breinged in, while the eagles watched, and the ravens flapped into birch branches, *kronking* and croaking. Borb flew down once to harass, and was almost caught by the lightning snap of Bodach's jaws. She did not try again.

So, with seven ravens watching, and two eagles waiting on, the badgers fed, not looking up or making haste. After they had gone, nine scavengers flew down, squabbling over the prey. And this time the eagles took possession.

Day after day the sun shone in a cloudless sky, and the air shimmered in the heat. Although it was cool in the tunnel under the scree, the badgers moved downhill to lie out aboveground in a bracken thicket close to the dead hind. While they were there it was eaten down to bones, sinews and skin, which woodmice and shrews nibbled at in the night.

One morning, long before sunrise, they heard the barking of dogs on the hill. It was coming closer, and was between them and their tunnel in the scree, so all they could do was wait, alert and prepared for what might be coming. The dogs were Border collies, and belonged to Pharic, who was close behind with two workers from the farm. They were on their way to gather the Ben Dearg sheep for the milk clipping, and wanted them down with their lambs in the morning coolth instead of the heat of the day.

Pharic's three dogs were good, tireless workers on the hill, and Liz, his senior bitch, had a mind for things other than sheep: she could stand to game like a setter. Predictably, she winded the badgers and stood to them, and Pharic thought there might be a fox in the bracken. One of the farm workers was carrying a shotgun, which he unslung from his shoulder and took from its scabbard. He loaded both barrels and Pharic waved Liz into the bracken.

Bodach and Mathair broke from cover when the bitch almost ran on top of them, taking the men by surprise and tempting two dogs to chase. 'Badgers!' exclaimed the farm worker, lowering and breaking his gun. Pharic whistled to the two dogs and they came skulking back to heel.

'Funny, lying there,' he said to the others, 'and them wi a hundred acres of rocks tae hide in.'

Chapter Seven

Rain clouds were lurking in the southwest, in ambush for the sun at its westering, when Pharic, with three dogs at heel, came round by the eagles' eyrie in the hot glare of late afternoon and sat down on top of the crag to spy the ground below and around. His ewes were back on the hill, whiter white and big-bellied after the clipping, shear-marked and freshly keeled with blue on their rumps. It was a somnolent day of fly buzz and no wind, and Pharic was in his shirt sleeves as they say, with his jacket as a back apron and the sleeves tied round his waist.

First he aimed the telescope down the scree, with the hill man's sure ability to pinpoint a selected spot at the first spy, and picked up the three wildcat kittens playing on a big rock, and in and out of a cleft, pouncing on each other and grappling as kittens do. It struck him at once that they were playing not far from where Liz had roused the badgers, and he decided to go down that way after he had spied along the Breac to the grass moor and round to the heather slope of Ben Dearg.

Although he had no idea that the voles on the grassland were at the peak of a four year cycle, swarming like maggots on a

76

carcass, he knew they were there. So he was not surprised to see a kestrel hovering and a pair of short-eared owls quartering the ground like setters. But it did surprise him to see Iolair – mightiest of the lordly ones – high stepping and flat footed, like a man wearing snowshoes, walking thigh deep in moor grass, dabbing for voles and gulping them down, like a buzzard catching worms after rain or a farm fowl seeking stubble grain.

Between the Piper's Cairn and the grouse moor another bird was hunting: a big bird, a twice sparrowhawk, gull-like, in plumage of silver – a cock hen-harrier. His mate, owl-faced like himself but in buskins of brown, was lying on her side in the shadow of a rock outcrop on the edge of the moor, with a wing and a leg outstretched and neck feathers on end, cooling off out of the sun's hot glare. Her four fledged young were nearby, burrowing for shade under the heather leafage: they were ready to fly and would soon be learning to hunt.

On the spurs and knolls above the moor red deer hinds were grazing with calves at foot. The spots of the earliest born calves were already greying: the later ones still had snowflaked flanks and hips. All of them were wagging ears, twitching tails, and shaking heads against the assault of female tabanid flies, now at their most aggressive, seeking from the deer the blood meal without which they could not produce eggs. Male tabanids, unlike the blood sucking females, are harmless feeders on plant juices and do not attack deer.

Pharic slapped the glass shut, called up the dogs, and started downhill. Twice on the way he stopped to view the wildcat kittens: at the first spying they were there, but at the second they were not to be seen. The dogs found the entrance to the den, and Liz was eager to explore, but he called them off and held away to The Spoot where they quickly found the remains of the hind: skin, hair, skull, and bones with dark stains and shrivelled sinews. Pharic was puzzled by the broken birch branch until he noticed the deer hair in the cleft, when he made a shrewd guess at what had happened.

The dogs wanted to run through the bracken, and he had to speak to them sternly to keep them wide: *Liz! Mirk! Ben! Come*

77

oot o that! Liz, the huntress, was the sweirtest to come to heel. She remembered the badgers, and either knew or guessed that they were again lying in the bracken. Bodach and Mathair, dozing a few yards apart in the shady warmth, came alert when they heard the man's voice, but did not stir, and Pharic had no wish to disturb them. He too guessed they were there. The dogs followed him reluctantly across the face of the hill towards the moor. He was well down towards the Slainte flats when he spied a lone ewe and he knew, by her behaviour, that she had lost her lamb. She stamped with a foot, and bleated, when she saw him coming on with the dogs.

She was standing over her dead lamb, among rocks at the base of a small cliff with twisted rowans and aspens growing along the top and outwards from vertical fissures. The lamb had fallen from the top – a drop of twenty feet to the rocks below. Hoodie crows had already pecked out its eyes, and had been probing into the body under the tail.

Burying his dead was ritual with Pharic, not only because he was required by law to do so, but because unburied bodies might encourage carnivores to take too great an interest in lamb or mutton. That day he was without the entrenching tool he usually carried strapped to his back pack at lambing time, but it would have been useless anyway for digging a grave in the hard, gravelly ground. So he hefted the lamb's body to a shallow under a boulder, where wild thyme grew, and laid it there. He built a low cairn of stones over it, then dragged two heavy rocks into position and wedged them firmly to form an outer shield against grave robbers. He was sure that no fox, attracted by the smell of lamb, would be able to move them.

'You'd as well be awa now, woman,' he said to the ewe. 'Your lammie'll no be coming back.'

With the dogs at heel he made haste at the hill man's deceptive slow-walk to the Piper's Cairn, and from there spied the wide sweep of moor grass, where the entrances to the vole creeps were like dark eyes peering from the tussocks. Iolair, three hundred yards away and still hunting voles, saw him before he sat down, and ran wing-flapping and high-stepping

78

like a swan taking off from water. He needed a clearway below him before he could fly, and knew exactly where he was going. Pharic watched him hop-flapping on to a rocky knoll, where wheatears nested, and from there launch away, out and across the Slainte, then up and round towards Ben Dearg.

Frayed feathers of cloud, detached from ambush, were skirmishing towards the sun, and the dogs began to pant, wide-mouthed, with carnassials showing and hot tongues dripping sweat. A wandering whidder of wind, not enough to stir a hair on the dogs, was like their breath on Pharic's face, and he looked at the sky, sensing a weather change.

He was rising to go when he saw Coll with Sgian on the Ben Dearg scree, coming his way, and decided to wait for him. A dark brown butterfly settled on the rock beside his feet when he sat down again. It was a Scots Argus, like a cut-out in velvet, with a copper band on fore and hindwings, and on each band three dark eyes with highlights. Pharic knew the butterfly without being able to put a name to it. A cloud feather veiled the sun and it flew from the rock into hiding; when the cloud passed it took wing again, with others of its kind. The Argus is a sun lover, but its caterpillars, which feed on moor grass, come out only at night.

Many of the butterflies were a-wing when Coll came up fifteen minutes later, with a stalking rifle under his arm and Sgian at heel.

'I saw you and waited on,' Pharic greeted him. 'Was that you fired the shot a while back?'

'It was indeed,' Coll laughed. 'Simon got word there was some big foxes in the bracken ayont The Spoot. I got one.' He pulled a brush from his game bag. 'A young one.'

'This year's model, and big,' Pharic said.

'Yes, and there was anither two. We've had a flitting on to us we could hae done without. By heck! Can you see their faces come the twelfth if we start driving foxes in wi the grouse?'

'It's been kent,' Pharic grinned. 'But tell me: did you have Sgian through the bracken this side o The Spoot? There's a pair o badgers lying out there.'

79

'A pair? There was three. And guess what? One of them was the one you keeled a while back – the one we patched up.'

'Well, well, well!' Pharic said, interested. 'There was only the pair when Liz put them up the day before the gathering.'

'Well, there's three there now, and they gave Sgian a wee bit of an argument before they broke out and into the scree. There's a den there.'

'You'd wonder what brings them away oot here,' said Pharic. 'And what they get to eat.'

'I've often wondered that myself,' Coll admitted. 'But at least we ken now where one of them is from, and likely the other two forbye. It's always in July month they're here, and then they're awa again before The Twelfth. The terriers never find a sniff o them after that. I expect thur three would have their share o the dead beast at The Spoot.'

'You found it then?'

'Sure. Hanged itself, looks like. But I could see no cats.'

'That'll be right. I came that way with the dogs and Liz was at the den.'

Clouds on a wide front were now advancing towards the sun, and the wind freshening. Rain was not far away, and likely a storm. Out of habit the men spied the Slainte before leaving for home. Across the river, beyond the boundary, they saw Colin Campbell crouched beside one of his gins, and by the actions of him they knew he was working on something with a gralloching knife. When he rose they saw him stuffing something grey into his game bag.

'That bliddy man . . .' Coll muttered, shaking his head. 'That'll be anither badger he's got. Sure as daith that's where Keely copped it.'

'You could be right,' Pharic agreed, his face expressionless. 'We should be in the sporran business.'

Three badgers lay up in the sanctuary of their rock citadel, alert and listening, until long after Coll and Sgian had gone. Then they fell asleep – Bodach with his forepaws covering his eyes,

Mathair cheek to flank, and Keely with her nose tucked into her chest. Soon Bodach was snoring, twitching in sleep. Mathair rolled over on to her back, and lodged against him, fingering her belly fur with her foreclaws.

The storm broke with a cloudburst and the badgers could hear the drum roll of rain on the rocks; but they slept on, hearing without heeding. It fell in steady downpour, and the hill's dried-out arteries pulsed again with water – seeping, bubbling, trickling, gushing and leaping. The Spoot surged down white-crested, rioting and pounding in the gorge, and carried away the clean-picked bones of the dead hind along with debris of woodrush, birch and heather. Ben Dearg, with the lightning flaring and flickering in its mushroom smother of clouds, became a volcano erupting. The thunder cracked as though it would split the sky, then rumbled away to a death rattle.

For fifteen minutes the storm's artillery flashed and thundered. Then came the wind. It skelloched and ranted to a gale, driving the rain across the slope and the red deer to the lee side of Ben Dearg. Sheep and lambs, staggering in the gusts, trooped to the shelter of knolls and rocks and hollows. One lamb, following its mother along a path across the eagles' crag, was lifted by the gale and rolled downhill. It scrambled back to the path, unhurt, but instead of forking right after the ewe it leaped across a narrow chasm – into the eyrie! And there it was trapped, bleating, with the ewe *baa-ing* above. There was no way out for it except by the way it had come; but because the ewe was ahead, as well as above, it had no thought of turning back.

Before midnight the storm slackened. The wind's rant died away; the rain became a drizzle, then a cat's purr; and when the cloud cover opened the moon was there, full and bright in a clear sky.

It was still riding high, westering, when Bodach left the den. He scratched himself vigorously – flanks, neck and belly – then sniffed into the cool wind, now gentled to a steady blow that barely lifted the hair of his thatch. Mathair and Keely joined

81

him syne, and they played in threesome near the rocks, avoiding the sodden bracken. The wildcats appeared on the rocks above, unsheathed their claws, stretched themselves, then padded up the scree and away. When Mathair and Keely, tiring of the play, wandered off towards The Spoot, Bodach went back to bed. He was not yet hungry enough to face a drenching from soaked grass and heather.

An hour and a half before sunrise he came out and padded across the hill towards the Piper's Cairn, following a well-trodden deer path along which he left a trail of five-clawed tracks clearly printed on the wet surface. Few voles were moving in the grass, which was still sowpit in the deeps and quickly sleeked the black hair of his legs and belly. A long-eared owl was hunting there, but not flying with its usual assured buoyancy because its feathers were still raggled with wet. Twin green orbs, luminous but not moving, betrayed an alerted fox beside the cairn; but Bodach, with the wind behind him, was receiving no signals. So he shambled slowly on, pinned down a fat vole, and swallowed it with some grass. It was then he saw the fox, snarling and flashing teeth in threat.

The fox was a dog – big-framed, leggy and strong – with a fine thick brush and four years of wisdom in his head: the same fox that had bloodied his face in the body of the dead hind at The Spoot. He had no more notion of seriously challenging a badger than he had of researching gin traps or looking down the barrels of a twelve-bore. But that morning he was thinking that the vole patch beside the cairn was his own, and he resented the badger's intrusion. So he was prepared to demonstrate, to threaten with flash of ivory from a safe distance.

Bodach, unconcerned, ignored him and prowled on, rooting in the tussocks, some of which, undercut by the nibbling of voles, came away like swathes on his face. When the fox feinted towards him, with show of teeth, threatening from a safe distance, he tucked his head between his forepaws, and waited, on guard but not yet roused to anger. The demonstration, so far, he was prepared to put up with. But when the fox closed in, snapping, and paw-whipped him on the rump, he had had enough. Up came his head, and he struck out – dart, dart – with teeth bared and a growl in his throat. The darting arrowhead, and the terrible teeth, daunted the fox; he back-tracked and trotted off to look for another and safer vole patch. That was the wisdom of him, and why he was four.

From the cairn Bodach hunted out towards The Corrach, snapping up Scots Argus caterpillars which were feeding on moor grass, and killing two more voles. Between vole kills he met, one after the other, three young self-hunting stoats from Fraioch's family, dispersing in search of territories of their own: all were males. A big dog stoat, now running with their mother, had taken over the Breac territory and driven them out after mating with their sisters. The sisters were still at the Breac; the other two dog kits had taken the high road to the cut-over wood.

Bodach left the grass moor and followed the Slainte flat to the heather, eating earthworms and a frog on the way. In the heather he caught an emperor moth and caterpillars, and put to flight one of the young hen-harriers while it was flapping its wet wings to dry. The bird flew across the moon's face and wheeled to pitch on the cliff from which Pharic's lamb had fallen to its death. Bodach hunted up and round to the cliff, taking the shortest route to the scree because the light was coming up in the east. At the bottom of the cliff his nose found the place where Pharic had buried the lamb.

The wedged rock slabs that were proof against foxes were no obstacle to a powerful boar badger and he soon had one removed. He pulled down the second, clawed away the stones of the little cairn, and dragged the body of the lamb into the open. Beetles were crawling on its body, and where it had been lying, and he ate them. But, perhaps because there was little hunger in him, he ate little of the lamb, taking only a small piece from the neck and leaving the rest. Thus he made available to other carrion eaters what Pharic had hoped to keep away from them.

The sun was up, in cocoon of white cloud, when he arrived back at the den, where Mathair and Keely were squatting, licking their bellies and legs. Bodach sniffed them, scented them on their rumps, and joined them, being wet himself to his grey-line. Then he went to bed. When the sun, escaping from its opaque cocoon, flooded the scree with light and warmth, all three came out again and lay at the entrance to the den, facing in, their eyes closed in half sleep but their ears and noses alert. So they heard the footsteps of Coll while he was yet some way off, and bolted into the den without waiting for a smell of him.

Coll had with him his big retriever Sgian, and the terriers Tarf and Sionnach. Tarf, her wounds long healed, was her old tireless, varminty self, and that day her mind, like Coll's, was on foxes. Coll was carrying a rifle, and had the terriers with him just in case. Foxes on foot were not their business, but one never knew what might happen. Sgian he had out for the exercise, muscling him up for the grouse season, now only eight days away.

Within earshot of the badgers Coll stopped to spy the eagles' eyrie: out of habit, nothing more, for he knew better than anyone how long the young birds had been on the wing. So he was surprised and puzzled when he saw something white there – white like an eaglet where he knew no eaglet was. He quickly realised that the white thing was a lamb, and when he raised the glass he saw the ewe on the trackway above. 'Good God!' he exclaimed, making the dogs prick their ears. Then he thought: *silly bitch o a yowe: how the hell did she get her lammie in there?*

Forgetting about foxes he palmed the glass shut, called in the dogs, and started up the edge of the scree, feeling bound to do something about the lamb. The climb was steep, and he went up in short zig-zags, making haste slowly, stopping only once when the terriers put on foot a well grown wildcat kitten which they wanted to follow into the rocks. At his sharp command, which he had to give twice, they came back reluctantly, with birses up and tails down, and Coll laughed quietly, reading the signs. The birses were for the cat; the tails down for the reprimand they expected and did not get.

He followed the lamb's path to the eyrie and viewed it from the edge of the chasm, which was nearly three feet wide. The chasm was no more than a split in the crag, going down tapering and sheer for six feet to a grassy slope ending at the head of the scree. After prodding the edge of the eyrie with his stick to make sure it was firmly based, he ordered the dogs down below the path, steadied himself and leaped across. The lamb panicked, bleating, and ran to the far edge of the eyrie, and for a moment he feared it might jump off into space. It would almost certainly do that, he thought, if he tried to turn it back by the way it had come. So he reached at it with his stick. He succeeded, with one try, in catching it by the neck with the crook, pulled it to him, and gathered it in his arms.

It was a big lamb, and strong, and he had difficulty holding it. It kicked and struggled, and its terrified bleating started the ewe *baa-ing*, and rushing backward and forward on the path above, like a dog on a running chain. At first Coll thought of jumping from the eyrie with the lamb under an arm; instead he decided to throw it. Grasping it by its neck and rump wool, he held it head forward like an osprey carrying a fish, swung it, then threw it across to the path. It fell on its face, rolled downhill a few feet, righted itself, and was back on the path facing him when he leaped the chasm after it.

But instead of running on it was determined to come back and Coll had to call up the terriers to make a display in front of him. Their barking and mock threats frightened it, and turned it, and the ewe, knowing where it was, bounded sure-footed down to join it. It kneed down on the spot, reached under and suckled, punching her udder with its nose. Coll, who could never resist thinking words, or speaking them to animals, said to it:

'It's a good thing for you this isn't June month, or you'd be lamb chops by this time.'

With the dogs gathered he now hurried downhill, following the edge of the scree; he had lost time and was anxious to be at the place where he had already killed a fox. When he saw Bodach's fresh tracks on the deer path he oxtered both terriers and carried them past the den, outside which were many other betraying five-clawed prints. He had to hold tightly on to Tarf, because her nose was owning the smell of badger and she wanted to be free. Coll spoke sharply to her, and held on, content to carry her as far as need be from the attraction of the badger magnetism.

Inside the den Bodach was sitting up, facing out; Mathair and Keely had moved deeper into the rocks. He guessed that the man had gone, and the dogs with him, but he held his place, facing the daylight, not alarmed yet not at ease, with his ears hearkening and his nose asking questions. Not knowing what to expect, he was ready for the unexpected.

One hundred and fifty yards from the den Coll put the terriers down and called to them to follow on. Sionnach followed without argument, along with the steady, unquestioning Sgian, but the volatile Tarf, already half on the boil, broke away back to the scree, at a speed incredible in a small, short-legged dog. Coll roared after her: *Tarf!* He whistled the recall. She looked back once then carried on, a victim suddenly of the deafness that sometimes afflicts working terriers. She was into the rocks, and facing Bodach, almost before Coll was in his stride in pursuit.

In the near-dark of the tunnel all Tarf could see was the white of the badger's face. She breasted down, with her rump high and her tail gay, and barked at him – a harsh, girning bark that skirled in the tunnel and shocked the badger's sensitive ears. But Bodach did no more than stand up, with his chin down, rumbling in his chest, without threatening move or show of aggression. He had plenty of room and was content to wait. Tarf quickly realised there was no way for her past that fearsome black-and-white Bydand sign, and barked the more furiously: prancing, darting, feinting right and left, taunting him. But he was not to be drawn. Then Coll, with head and shoulders in the entrance, blocking out the light, was calling to her:

'Tarf! Tarf! D'ye hear? Come oot o that, you stupid little bitch! Tarf! Dammit, dug, is it anither pasting you're asking for?'

Tarf heard, and when she half turned to lend an ear Bodach made a sudden strike at her, not following through, and she back-tracked her length to keep clear of him. Bodach brumbled away, shaking his head now like a bear, while Coll continued calling her, urgently, and syne angrily: 'Tarf! Come to me dammit! By heck I'll sort ye!' At that point discipline overcame the wilfulness in her and she drew off far enough to let him grab her by the tail and pull her out. He backed out and rose to his feet, holding her by the tail at arm's length, and slapped her twice on the rump, once with the back of his hand and once with the palm. Then he put her down and ordered her to follow him.

He rated her no more than that. Although he liked his terriers well in hand, he also liked the devil in them, and believed that the cutting edge of their courage could be blunted by too much manning. Tarf followed him, almost meekly, with her tail down but her mind still on the badgers. Presently, however, trotting with Sionnach behind Coll and the placid Sgian, she forgot and her tail went up again.

That night, long before sunset, with grouse *backing* and a buzzard mewing high in the glare, Bodach took his incoming morning trail back to the cliff where he had left the lamb. There was little left of it now – head, neck bones and some wool – to attract anything bigger than shrews or mice, or perhaps a ring ouzel or a jackdaw. Foxes had eaten from the carcass at first light; Fior-eun the eagle had carried away the hindquarters; and the ravens Pruk and Borb had picked the remainder almost clean during the day. They were still on the cliff when Bodach arrived, clawing their beaks, shaking their feathers, and rubbing ears against wing-elbows. They made guttural comment when he sniffed over the remains, but he ignored them and turned away downhill.

Along the Slainte he snapped up beetles and caterpillars, and a water shrew which he surprised nibbling a snail beside a dub of water in an alder thicket. Black grouse were roosting in the riverside trees. At moonrise, on the grass moor, he began to hunt voles, and caught two in half an hour. There he found the scents of Mathair and Keely and set his own beside them. Near the Piper's Cairn he found a dead stoat, still warm, which he touched with his nose and turned over with a forepaw. It was one of Fraioch's kits, killed by the big dog fox when it was

87

carrying a vole into hiding to eat it. The fox had eaten the vole but had no stomach for stoat: Bodach sniffed it then cuffed it aside with a paw, having no inclination to eat it.

By the time the moon was high he had a full stomach and wanted to sleep: no badger, unhungry, prowls the night through for exercise. In a rock niche under the Piper's Cairn he found a couch of bedstraw and lay down on it, with his chin on his belly and a forepaw over his face. From somewhere near The Corrach the whooping of Sealgair the tawny owl came faintly to his ears, and once his nostrils twitched to the taint of the dog fox whose footfalls he could not hear. He showed no reaction when a swallow-like bird, garbed like an owl, pitched on the cairn to rest for a moment, sitting not standing. The bird was a nightjar, with wide-cleft mouth bristled like a fly-trap. It uttered a soft *churr* and flew silently away. Bodach heard the *churr*.

When he awoke the moon was far across the sky, hazed in a spider's web of cloud. He shook himself, scratched his neck, then slow-trotted across the grass moor towards The Corrach: for the time being be would not be returning to the den in the scree. It was a temporary away-from-home den which he would have left within the next few days in any case. Tarf's visit made the decision for him to move out earlier.

At the bridge of larch planks over the Breac he turned from the trail into a thicket of raspberry canes, where he began feeding on the ripe fruit, clawing sprays to his mouth or picking single berries with his teeth. With them he chewed and swallowed some leaves. Mathair and Keely were already there; he could smell them, and hear them moving among the raspberry canes. When he could no longer hear them he knew they had gone, and soon afterwards he followed them, taking the well concealed trail from the bridge to The Corrach sett.

Bough! Bough!

No dog bark this, or yap of fox: it was the chesty bass of a mature roebuck, with fires stoked for the rut. Bodach stopped for a moment, with ears hearkening and a forepaw raised, then he padded on. He knew what it was: it was part of the fabric of the night and the season, without special meaning for him, and he was content to listen and go on his way. But, suddenly, the beast was there on the trail, coming towards him – Boc-earb, the master buck of The Corrach, with the spring in his legs and top tines like ivory dirks. And no badger was going to make him turn aside.

Bodach left the trail, porpoised through the ground cover in a curving detour, and rejoined it behind the buck. Boc-earb minced on without looking back, having as little interest in badgers as they had in him. At the sett Mathair and Keely were seated beside one of the four entrances, grooming their fur. Bodach sniffed them over in greeting and lay down nearby to lick the pads of his forepaws. At daylight Caileag arrived, and soon afterwards her cubs: the three had never left The Corrach sett. Rain came with daylight and six badgers went to ground there.

The following night six badgers left, but only Caileag and her cubs returned. The other three were back at home in the Breac sett.

Chapter Eight

Mathair, first home, found a stranger at the sett – a young boar in his second year: a vagrant from across the Slainte, in search of a friendly clan or an unpaired sow.

It was his mate that Coll and Pharic had watched Colin Campbell taking from the trap, in which she had been lying all night, and throughout the furnace heat of the day before, and most of the night before that. The young boar had kept tryst with her during two darknesses, straying from her only on brief forays to snatch a hasty bite, and on the day between he had denned alone, for the pair were the only badgers on Ardcreag. On the second morning, finding her exhausted, weak and unresponsive, and with a strange fear in him, he left her at first light and broke a new trail to the river, not setting scent because he had no thought of returning.

Downstream from The Corrach he forded the Slainte, where it glissaded like a mill lade over its flat rock bed: a wanderer knowing why he was travelling but not where. On the Dalnabreac side he turned upstream, with head down, at an inswinging trot. In The Corrach he found the scent of Keely and her family, and at Ash Tree that of Mathair's cubs; but he kept on travelling, following the plain trail in the glen, and across the burn, to the Breac sett. Now, on the fourth morning, he was about to meet the returning Breac clan.

Homing across the wind and down from him, Mathair placed him by scent before he knew she was there, and stopped to ponder, arcing her muzzle with her nose asking questions. The wind told her he was male and a stranger. She squatted for a moment to set her usual scent marker for the clan: when she rose she released another scent, involuntarily, from her anal glands – a heavy odour of musk that betrayed her uncertainty and disquiet. Afraid, she would have released the same wave of musk – her funk smell as Coll would have said – but there was no fear in her. Back to her den she had to go, and there she was going, stranger or no stranger. She moved forward warily, lifting and laying each forepaw slowly, like a crouched fox stalking. The stranger still could not smell her, but presently he saw her.

He porpoised to her, his hindquarters swaying, in eager welcome; but she turned away from him snarling, refusing to let him set his scent on her, and thrust into her tunnel, where she turned about to face him, snapping at him when he began to purr. He was purring to her, trying to draw her, when Bodach came shambling up the slope.

Bodach rushed at him without warning, grabbed him savagely by the neck, and shook him. The young boar reared, and his attacker with him, and they lost footing and rolled downhill in close embrace, gathering leaf debris, sclaffing in the mould, and flattening momentarily the fern clumps. When they rolled to a stop Bodach still had him clawed by the shoulders – worrying him, mauling him, hurting him, and biting deeper and deeper. The young boar tried to fight back but he was helpless in Bodach's jaws, which were closed on his neck with immovable grip, like the lock-fast teeth of a steel trap. With such a grip on a small terrier he could have torn away half its neck. He could have inflicted almost as serious damage on the young boar, despite his thick fur and skin: instead, for some

91

reason, he released his hold and stood quietly aside, letting him run away.

He crossed the Breac, dripping blood on the stepping stones, and Bodach splashed after him to keep him moving; he had no intention of renewing the attack, and would not have followed him far. The young boar changed all that by turning about to face him squarely on the trail. Bodach bowled him over and snapped at his throat, getting his mouth full of fur but no grip on the skin. The young boar scrambled to his feet and, realising the hopelessness of his plight, fled at speed along the main Ash Tree trail. Bodach did not chase him farther: with the intruder driven off he had no more interest in fighting.

When Keely arrived home the three set scent on each other, then the sows went to ground for the day. Bodach clawed at the old bedding on the mound at the entrance to his tunnel, teased some loose and lost interest in it. He padded along the length of the sett, sniffing over every mound and at all the entrances, as though seeking another intruder. At the end of the line he found rabbit smell in a tunnel from which leaves had been scraped; the rabbits had moved in when the sett was deserted, and their purlies were scattered on the mound. Bodach pushed in to the end of the tunnel, and found that the rabbits had extended it with their own narrow burrows, into which he could not follow. He wasted no time digging and took the underground route to his bed.

Sunshine and a steady wind throughout the day dried out herbage and surface leaf litter, and when the badgers came out at dusk they spent the first hour gathering and carrying in new bedding. Bodach worked first at a fern clump, scooping fronds into a small bundle which he clasped under his chin with his forepaws and carried home backwards, elbowing his way over the mound. He went into his tunnel rear-end first and pulled it in after him. Mathair and Keely were gathering fireweed, or rosebay willow herb, from a stand in a clearing thirty yards from the west end of the sett, pulling the tall plants from their shallow root-hold with their teeth and scattering the feathery seedheads to the wind. Each carried two bundles to the den, held length-wise across their chests.

All three stopped gathering at the same time and wandered off on their separate ways for the rest of the night. In the morning they went straight belowground, gathering no bedding, perhaps because all the vegetation was soaked with dew. But at night they spent another hour collecting before moving out to hunt, leaving straggles of ferns, leaves, fireweed, dog's mercury and wild liquorice along the frontage of the sett.

At Drochaid Farm the corn was ripening; soon it would be ready for cutting. While Mathair and Keely took The Corrach trail to hunt voles in the moor grass, Bodach visited the cornfield, and for two hours he feasted on oats, breasting down the stalks and ripping off the ickers with his teeth. The night was warm, with the wind whispering in the corn and a horned moon westering: a tawny owl was hunting along the endrigg hedgerow. When he had stuffed himself with oats Bodach curled up to sleep in the corn, not stirring until after the moon had set. Then he ate more oats and left for home.

After that he was joined in the cornfield by Mathair and Keely, and for part of each night they fed on oats, while the horned moon, trailing the afterglow, waxed egg-shaped then full. Nothing disturbed them, and the only sounds were the rustle of ripe corn, the whiplash calls of the hunting owl and the barking of dogs at Drochaid Farm.

Then Drummond began cutting, and in a day the field was bare except for rows of straw. Drummond knew the badgers had been there, because they had trampled and touzled about a tenth of an acre of his ten-acre field, and along the hedge he found many of their scats which were stiff with oats and husks and looked like corn dollies. One morning he found dead and dying wasps on the flattened stalks where Bodach had rolled to rid his coat of them after pulling out their bike from under a hedgerow elm.

Once the field was cleared all that was left for the badgers was stubble grain, which was unrewarding work, and when they visited it after the harvest it was to look for earthworms and slugs, or snatch an unwary woodmouse from the hedgebottom, where they also dug for pig-nuts and roots. Drummond of Drochaid often wondered about these diggings and thought the badgers were hunting mice. It would have surprised him even more to learn that they were also nibbling clover and wild parsley, eating raspberries, and sometimes a ripe, glossy doghip.

These were nights of plenty for the Breac clan, when they began to lay on fat for the long slow-burn of winter. It was also the wasp season, when the bikes were at their peak of strength and the combs crammed with succulent grubs: when man shot grouse by day and badgers wrecked the fiery fortresses at night.

The first bike Bodach dug out was the one above Caileag's old nursery, which now had seven tiers of well filled comb with pepper pillars between: it was bigger than the biggest swede turnip ever grown on Drochaid. With his powerful bear claws he scraped out earth, stones and roots, and scooped out the paper citadel, wrecking its scalloped shell and scattering the fragments downhill and around. Ignoring the wasps he began to munch the combs, swallowing paper with the grubs. The wasps were lethargic and crawled about on the ground among the wreckage. Some crawled up Bodach's legs and into his fur; others reached his face and he brushed them away with a forepaw. One stung him on the nose, which seemed to bother him a little; he licked it in and ate it.

Wrecking wasps' bikes became a nightly affair, and Bodach dug out three more, as well as the cocoons from two bumble bee nests, within a week. Seeing the wreckage at the Breac sett on the Sunday, when he was out walking with Pharic, Coll said:

'It's funny. You think you ken a lot of wasps' bikes till the badgers get to work on them. Then you see how many of them you've missed. Look at this lot. They must've kent about it all along, but they've left it till it was full o meat!'

'Makes sense,' Pharic said. 'We do the same wi the tatties and the neeps!'

One morning, after hunting voles on the grass moor, Bodach was homing through The Corrach in the gusty dawn when he came on Boc-earb, the master buck, with a doe in a clearing. He was chasing her, withershins, in a tight circle round a pine stump, and they had worn out a path as plain as a badger run. The buck's tongue was showing and the doe's mouth open. Bodach halted momentarily – viewing dimly, hearing clearly, and recognising by smell – then padded on without interest or concern, unaware that his trail was overlapped by their rutting ring. Ordinarily, the deer's reaction to a passing badger would have been to stand and stare; but Boc-earb was no ordinary buck, and when Bodach cut a chord on his circuit he gave chase.

Bodach bolted, with back thatch flapping, alarmed and not asking questions, and found refuge behind a pine tree. He was at a loss to understand such behaviour for roebucks, even at the height of the rut, are not given to chasing badgers or anything else. In Boc-earb the rutting fire was dying, which made his behaviour all the more inexplicable. But there was still a spark in him, and he lunged at Bodach, buckling at the knees and stabbing forward and up with his dirks. When Bodach moved round the tree he stabbed at the trunk where he had been, grunting and pawing a scrape with a forehoof. Then, suddenly, he lost interest, and stepped back, shaking his head and looking right and left. Placing the doe he paraded towards her, with chin down and antlers at the present, and began to run her again on the ring. After that experience Bodach paid attention when he heard him *boughing* in the wood.

The grouse shooting season was at its peak but it was a daytime activity, far away, and the badgers knew nothing of it. Nor did they see or hear anything of the people who shot over the moor because they travelled from Drochaid Farm to the far side of Ben Dearg. Only once that season, when the ponies and Land Rovers were returning late, did a party see Keely crossing the road. When the headlamps dazzled her one of the party broke his gun to load it but Coll, sitting in the back with Sgian, and up to the knees in dead grouse, snapped at him: 'Hold on! We don't shoot badgers here!' Keely crashed through the roadside fence into the field, and when Coll said he knew her the man *haw-hawed* and did not believe him. Nor did he notice that Keely was a blue-back.

During the grouse season the badgers had their regular, but flexible, routine. On dry nights they spent part of their time hunting voles on the grass moor, but after rain they went first to Drochaird where earthworms would be surfacing or drowning in puddles. Bodach was on his way there, after rain, on a night of lop-sided moon and drifting goose-feather clouds, when he found his last wasp bike of the season.

It was in a holly tree off the trail: a small bike half the size of the one at the sett – a tree wasp fortress hanging from a branch like an unlit lantern, its slate-blue shell not scalloped but ringed with ripples. It was too high for Bodach to reach it standing, so he climbed to it, shaking the tree without dislodging it. The holly leaves were toothless, not pricking, and the climb was easy for him. When he was level with the bike he shook the branch from which it hung, but it withstood his shaking as it had many a wind and gale. In the end he had to reach to it and claw it loose, and it fell, not shattering when it hit the ground. Bodach backed down and ripped it open, scattering curved layers of its shell. He devoured the combs, leaving only a few grubs to die in their hexagonal cells, shook invading wasps from his fur, and plodded on his way to Drochaid.

At the ride he found the familiar ground changed. Ten wooden huts had been erected inside the fence of the small inbye pasture where cows and calves had grazed earlier in the year, and where a calf had lost its tongue in a snare. Six cottages were to be built there, and Drochaid would lose half the pasture. The ride was to be cleared for an access road. Already, near the huts, were a bulldozer, a cement mixer, two dumper trucks, and a mound of bricks and concrete slabs. Long joists of timber were piled across the badger trail.

Bodach left the age-old badger trail to circle the pile of timber, and crossed the inbye into the big pasture where an Aberdeen Angus bull was running with fifteen cows and heifers. There, when searching for worms, he had turned over many a dung pat without arousing more than curiosity in the grazing cattle, although sometimes young beasts would follow him playfully. But this was a new bull, two years old, and he was not placid.

They will tell you, those who know, that the Angus is usually a quiet, easygoing beast, with no vice in him, and they are right to be sure; but once in a while there is the one that can be as unchancy and unpredictable as any dairy bull. As the cattle man said: *they're generally quate, but whiles you get a mean wan, and a mean Angus can be a proper bugger!* This bull was a mean one in the sense the word is used in the land of the double negative.

He was cudding when Bodach entered the field, all gluey muzzled and spittley, and big bellied with comfort forbye; but when he saw the badger in the field he kneed to his feet and stood for a moment, with his head down and swaying. He was flat-backed and square-ended, a gey bull of quality, with the Canada bit in him. He pawed the sod and bellowed; then he charged. Bodach heard the thud of his hooves, and was almost caught off guard, because he had had hoof thuds following him many a time. He let the bull almost on top of him before he bolted and ducked under the fence out of danger. The bull furrowed to a stop, roaring, butting and boring at the wire, while Bodach ran on, having had enough of the pasture for the night.

Downstream from Drochaid bridge he splashed across the Breac where it crept in wavelets over pebbles, dimpling and rippling the image of the lop-sided moon. After his fright he wanted to rest and he slept in a fern clump under a windfall until the moon was far down the sky and its reflection gone from the shallows. When he awoke his legs and belly fur were still wet and he licked himself and scratched before leaving for home. A tawny owl, perched on the top roots of the windfall with one foot drawn up into her feathers and a vole under the other, lifted long-legged away, startled, when she saw the badger rising from the fern clump.

Being a badger he foraged all the way along his homeward trail, which followed the high bank of the Breac as far as the

97

firwood. Twice he left it to rummage in hazel thickets, and once he rolled on a carpet of enchanter's nightshade near the edge of the burn; when he rose from the carpet he had hooked seeds clinging to his back. At the firwood he caught a small rabbit, which he carried into the dark tree cover to eat. He left a piece of skin with some flesh attached. After he had gone a questing water shrew found it, sniffed it all over with its trunk-snout, and feasted on it.

The morning was greying, and the wind freshening, breathing threat of rain, when he reached the head of the downhill trail to his crossing place. Across the burn, on a flat below the sett, Boc-earb was thrashing meadowsweet with his antlers and tossing the seedheads; on an oak branch above him two hoodie crows were yarring and stabbing at their perch. Bodach was halfway across and down the slope when he heard the whistle – a single piercing note no longer than a breath. It had come from the dark pool below him, upstream from his crossing place, where a bitch otter was playing with two well grown cubs.

Black shaking shadows of trees lay across the pool with a lane of reflected sky between. The otter swam across the sky lane and climbed on to one of his stepping stones, a flat boulder mossed in the cracks; her cubs stayed in the shadows, floating with only their crowns and nostrils showing above the water. On the boulder the otter sat tall, as stoats and weasels do, with her head to one side and her forepaws held to her chest: she was listening. Seal-sleek and sheened she was, sinuous and stream-lined – the river spirit that can do nothing gracelessly – and that morning, in the pallid dawn-light, she was an ebony sculpture in silhouette, on a plinth that was a badger's stepping stone.

She knew the badger was there, but perhaps not what he was, while Bodach, not seeing her, had already identified and placed her with his nose. For almost a minute she held her upright listening pose then, still alert, she dropped to all fours and trailed her dark length across the boulder, with her whiskered face close to the water on one side and her rudder clasping down on the other. Snake-like she glided from the boulder into the water, and swam back to the pool, where she nickered to her cubs to join her.

They were on their way to the Slainte, where the dog otter held five miles of the river and had a bigger range than Iolair the eagle. The bitch otter had killed two trout in the pool and shared them with her cubs, one of which had earlier made a great fuss over catching a lamprey, running ashore with it and refusing to let her brother touch it. The three were playing again when Bodach reached his stepping stones but they stopped when he was crossing, floating with only their nostrils and glossy pates showing, and watched him on the up-trail to the sett. The hoodies tore off leaves and Boc-earb trotted away when they saw him padding up the slope.

That day the otters lay up in the fireweed stand below the badger sett, sleeping fitfully between spells of hearkening to the sounds of the day – the yarring of crows, jays *squeching* in the oaks, the loud clap of cushat wings, the laughter of mallards on the Breac and the calling of a moorhen at the pool. They were gone when Bodach came out at darkening, and turned upstream for Drochaid; but Mathair saw them when she was crossing the bridge of planks from The Corrach. They were on the Slainte about the time Bodach entered the ride near Drochaid Farm by way of the swing gate in the larch wood fence.

The scene at the ride had changed further. The bulldozer had been at work throughout the day, and besides scooping out a great trench across the badger run had left spoilheaps like monstrous moleheaps, sprouting heather, foxgloves, ferns, grass and birch twigs. More bricks had been tipped in the pasture and drain pipes and roof tiles stacked along the fence.

Bodach made a detour round the end of the ditch and crossed the inbye. No cattle were grazing there now, but new straining posts were in position, and fence stobs laid out, to enclose the four acres being left to Drummond. For the rest of the night he foraged along the hedgerows – digging for pig-nuts, eating succulent heads of clover, snapping up beetles and earthworms, and trampling a trackway through wild parsley and hogweed, sneezewort and angelica. He was careful to stay out of the field where dwelt the Aberdeen Angus bull. The sun was coming up when he returned to the ride, so instead of continuing on his way home he holed up under the big beech tree where he had once been confronted by Drummond's Nell.

At half past eight in the morning, in light rain, the bulldozer started work on the bank where he was lying: the operator had come to dig out a length of it and pull down the tree. The monster stretched its neck, grabbed a mouthful of bank in its steel teeth, and passed it into its massive maw – a man-made dinosaur rending like *tyranosaurus rex*. Bodach felt the impact and came awake at once, alerted but not yet alarmed because he had no idea what was happening.

The monster turned away its head and spat out the mouthful, then swung back to take another bite, and another; and now Bodach crouched in fear, real fear, feeling the earth tremors and hearing the thud of the bites. But instead of bolting he began to dig – always his first reaction to intrusion – until suddenly, after the machine had taken more bites, the tree was toppling and he was being hoisted in the roots. Luckily the steel teeth did not touch him, and he sprackled clear of the debris when the load hit the ground and fled for the larch wood badger gate.

The operator, astonished at what he had excavated, stopped the machine. He recognised the beast as a badger, and although a townsman – perhaps because he was one – he was concerned that there might be others in the bank. So he went to find the foreman, with whom he discussed the matter, and in the end they were persuaded by one of the bricklayers, who was from the village, to send for Coll. But Coll was at the grouse, and would not be home until after dark. So they stopped the machine for the day, arranging that the bricklayer would see him at night.

At darkening Coll visited the spot with the bricklayer, knowing before he went that there was no sett in the ride – only one of the many temporary lying-up places the badgers had on Dalnabreac. But he felt he owed the workmen the visit when they had shown such consideration for the badger. For him it was a matter of what he called public relations.

'It's only a temporary place,' he told the bricklayer. 'There's no more badgers in it. But thanks for telling me, and say thanks for me to the foreman and the bulldozer chap. And now you'll have a dram with me before you go home?'

'That's the best offer I've had the day,' the bricklayer laughed.

Chapter Nine

These were hectic times for badgers and stalkers – the badgers gorging to put on more fat and the men turning from grouse to deer. The stalking season follows the grouse shooting, before the days of roaring, and it is then a stag's antlered head can be the death of him, for the man who pays to shoot him wants trophies not venison. Coll would be out every working day of the season – stalking, selecting the stag and directing the shooting.

But between the grouse and the stalking he had a few days to himself, and one clear night he made another visit to the badger sett above the Breac. There was an hour of light left and the moon was rising. There would be frost, he knew, so he was wearing his soft South Uist tweeds, felt boots, and a non-rustle parka, with a snood he could pull over his ears if they began to nip. The wind was blowing down the Breac, so he came in above the sett to his oak tree seat to keep his scent out of the badgers' noses. He climbed quietly into the oak, pulled the parka under him, and sat down on his usual branch to wait.

Three blackcocks were feeding in the burnside alders, filling their crops with young green cones and pecking at catkins. They had their lyre tails folded down; in the slanting light they were beetle-sheened ebony and Prussian blue. The white patches on their wing elbows were like staring eyes. Thus Coll saw them in his binoculars.

Once he was settled in the tree he sat still, moving only his head, and that slowly, when something attracted his attention. A jay, bright-eyed and most alert of birds, flew into a branch above him, shook its feathers and began to preen; then it saw the almost imperceptible lift of his head and flew *squeching* away. The tits knew he was there and scolded him, *churring* more in curiosity than alarm. Later, two hoodies flying into the next tree saw him before they had folded their wings, and lifted away again *cawing* harshly and spattering droppings on the oak-leaf carpet. Boc-earb, with a doe and her twins, came from behind, upwind, and passed below along the slope, not smelling the man because his scent was over their heads.

Badger light was nearing when Fraioch, the bitch stoat, came bounding slowly uphill with a vole in her mouth and disappeared into the burrow from which Bodach had dug the wasp bike. She now had a sleeping nest there to which she had added wasp paper. Although she made nightly contact with her mate – the dog stoat that had driven her kits from the Breac – she did not share her nest with him; he had a den of his own deeper in the oakwood.

The first badger out was Keely, and Coll smiled to himself for she was still as blue as a blackcock's neck in the sun. This made the fourth time he had seen her to recognise since the day he was sure he would never see her again. She sat on her mound for a minute or so, scratching herself, with her back to Coll, then she padded to the next one and thrust her head into the tunnel. When she pulled back another badger's face appeared at the entrance and presently Mathair joined her on the mound, where they backed up and scented each other.

It was then Coll saw the bobbing white arrowheads of two other badgers plodding up the trail from the stepping stones, their faces disappearing and reappearing in the thick ground cover. At first he thought they had been out before he arrived and were returning home early, for he guessed by the way

Mathair and Keely greeted them that they were members of the clan. What he could not know was that they were visiting members – Mathair's cubs from the Ash Tree sett. Now he had four badgers in close view, all clearly visible in good light.

The moon rose above the pine hackle across the Breac and the sett frontage was floodlit. A big rabbit, looking bigger than real in the moonlight, hopped down past the badgers' clawing post, and Coll was surprised that the four took no notice of it. They were still clambering over each other in a bourach, grunting and play-biting. At last Bodach looked out. He squatted at the entrance to his tunnel, not liking the moon full on his face, and not until the others were bounding across the mounds, playing a game like follow my leader, did he lumber out to scratch himself. Then he joined up with them.

They chased each other across the slope, and uphill and down, with Coll hearing more of them than he could see because of the thick ground cover of ferns, grass and brambles. They made as much noise as a stampeding flock of sheep, starting the hoodies talking at roost and sending below ground every foraging vole and woodmouse. Coll could hear them crashing in the fireweed, and see the downy seeds drifting in the moonlight.

But he was becoming confused, wondering just how many badgers were rampaging around in the thickets. One moment he was seeing two, and the next moment three; but not since the chasing started had he seen four or more together. Had some of them gone? He reckoned they had been roistering for more than two minutes, and wondered how much longer they would keep it up. He held his watch to the light to check the time, and when he looked up there was Bodach standing on his mound, motionless, looking downhill. And suddenly the chasing and the crashing stopped.

He watched and listened and saw nothing; then he looked down and there was Keely at the hole from which he had first seen her emerge after her release, so she must have come in from behind him. Now three more badgers were plodding uphill – Mathair and her two cubs – and that made the five he had seen before the playtime began. So they were all back. That was what he thought until another white arrowhead appeared on the uphill trail, followed by two more. The newcomers were Caileag and her cubs, and Coll had no idea when they arrived or by which way they had come. All he knew was that he now had eight badgers in front of him, in the clear moonlight, and easily counted.

The wind was now snell on Coll's face, and there was a chirp of frost in the grass. The least impatient of men, he was now beginning to wish the badgers would go away, not because he was losing interest in them but because he had already decided to come back before daylight to see how many came home in the morning. Bodach was the first to leave, taking the uphill trail; and Coll, wind-wise as a red deer, guessed what was likely to happen. The ground rose higher than the oak tree, so his scent would stot off the face and into the badger's nose, for the trail went behind him as well as up. And that is what happened. Bodach stopped as though he had walked into a fence and came bounding back to the sett, startling and scattering the sows and cubs. At the last moment he slowed pace and dived into his tunnel.

Before long he came out again and the clan began to disperse: one on the uphill trail and seven downhill. Three crossed the Breac and shuffled along the Ash Tree trail; two turned up-stream and two down on their own side of the burn. But their movements were hidden from Coll by the thick growth on the flat. The only badger he could recognise on sight was Keely, so he did not know if the beast padding uphill at confident pace was the same one as before. It was. Uphill was where Bodach wanted to go, and there he would go. Of course he walked into Coll's trapped scent again, but this time he did not break back: he walked through it, then bounded on his way.

He travelled to the cut-over wood where rabbits were grazing on grassy patches clear of the tangles of layered brashings. He passed them by without any attempt at chasing them, for alerted adult rabbits were beyond his coursing powers, and stalking them like a fox was not his style. Voles were also moving in the grass, but they were fewer than earlier in the year;

many were dying and some were already dead, for it is the destiny of voles not to know a second winter of life. Bodach picked up two of the newly dead, and ate them, then held away to the larch wood, through which he followed the lane-trail to the badger gate. In the ride he left the old, familiar runway, which still had timber lying across it and was even more cut up by the bulldozer than before. His mind was on the rich harvest of the Drochaid hedgerows.

The Aberdeen Angus bull, lying close to the hedgerow fence chewing cud, rose to his feet when he heard the badger on the other side. Bodach knew he was there because he could smell him, and hear him: the bulk of him was hidden by the thick hawthorn hedge. The bull snorted and sclaffed up divots with his hooves, sending them flying past his flank: his breath was vapour on the frosty air. Some of his cows lumbered up to stare with him and snort, but they soon lost interest and walked away. Bodach stopped at a bramble patch and began to pick berries. At the bottom of the field, on the same side of the hedge, a roebuck was also snipping berries, for the roe, like the badger, is a brambler.

Bodach had his own way with brambles. He picked off the lower berries standing, sat like a bear to reach those higher up, and poked carefully through the tendrils to reach clusters hiding in secret places in the grass. But always he picked them berry by berry, one at a time, which was not the way he picked raspberries. He had long ago learned that the bramble is spikier than the raspberry and pricks like a rose thorn.

When he had eaten all the brambles he wanted for one night he crossed the cornfield to the inbye hedge, sending a covey of partridges exploding across the moon's face on the way. He stopped, with a forepaw raised, when they burst from the stubble, listening to the whirr of wings, then shambled on his leisurely way. Skylarks fluttered from his path, and peewits, rising in a hushed storm of wings, mounted in close flock towards the moon, keening in protest.

Near the spot where he had found the calf's tongue a fat male hedgehog was eating a frog in a bramble patch. It was still alive

106

and he was eating it hindleg first. He was biting into its abdomen when he heard the tread of Bodach's pads on the frosted ground, and he coiled into a ball: by then the frog was dead. Turning himself into a barbed ball was his defence against enemies. But his hedgehog defences were of no avail against a determined badger, whose claws are a *schwerpunkt* without aid of teeth, and Bodach scooped him from the bramble patch, with a length of straw trailing from his back quills. He stayed coiled, and perhaps he felt secure.

With the deftness of the expert Bodach pawed the armoured ball until the chink in its armour was uppermost, the place where the hedgehog had his nose tucked into his feet, with his teeth still locked in a dead frog. Bodach started on the chink with his foreclaws, opening it wider and bleeding the hedge-hog's nose; then he tore it apart, with the ease of a man scooping a hole in garden soil with his fingers. The hedgehog was dead long before he had ripped the body completely open. He ate the remains of the frog, then the hedgehog down to the quills, one of which he swallowed by accident.

Between the cornfield and the farm were two more fields, the nearer under swedes on which Drummond would later fold his sheep. The other was down to potatoes for the market, with a few drills of Golden Wonders at the farm endrigg, grown specially for the Drochaid kitchen. Drummond could practise modern farming with the best but he never allowed himself to become the victim of it. He knew the kind of potato he wanted, and with muck and mysticism he grew it.

Bodach wandered into the swedes which were fat-bellied and gleaming – brawsome things with big leaves almost closing canopy between the drills. Partridges fed in the field each day, running head down between the drills, and that morning some had died, crumpled in a breath of gunsmoke and staining the green leaves with their blood. Bodach found a partridge, killed by one of Drummond's neighbours who was shooting without a retriever. It was the first partridge he had ever found. He plucked it with his teeth but ate little of it, for there is a limit to what a big badger can hold, even in the days of gorging. Unlike a fox he had no thought of carrying the bird home. Scraping soil over it he left it, which was the best he could think of.

From the swede field he pushed under the fence to the inbye and spring-trotted along the ride, picking his way round frosted puddles and glaur, avoiding machines, great mounds of whin chips, and other impedimenta of road-making. At his torn up cross-trail he turned into the cornfield again, where he found a heap of unbaled straw: he bored into it, curled up, and went to sleep. When he awoke the moon had gone and daylight was still some time off; but he set out for home and was in the cut-over wood when Coll was climbing into the oak tree to wait for him and his clan.

Coll had taken great care about his approach, mostly because he had no wish to scare the badgers, but also because he wanted every homing beast to come on to be counted. So he approached the sett from above, reckoning that seven badgers, if they did return, would come from below. The uphill trail troubled him more, for he expected the outgoing badger to return the same way, and he had to be careful about leaving his fresh foot scent across it. At the top of the slope he pulled a pair of old outsize stockings over his boots, stepped over the runway, and walked to the oak tree in them. He had soaked them in deer fat before leaving home . . .

The wind was from the east, blowing up the glen, which meant that his scent would be carried from the oak tree towards the sett; but he was sure it would be far enough above the ground to stay out of the badgers' noses, unless there came a gust to make a down draught. That was a chance he had to take. And he reckoned that any badger, winding him so close to home, would dive into the sett rather than run away. So he should see them all, however the wind behaved.

The frost was light but persisting; skin deep without cranreuch. The oak leaves were rustling like ripe corn. Across the Breac the pine hackle was a black silhouette against a brightening sky in which the stars were fading. Four white faces syne came bobbing uphill, and four badgers shambled on to a mound and disappeared into the sett: they were Mathair's and Caileag's cubs and had met at the stepping stones on the other side of the burn. Five minutes passed, and ten, then Mathair appeared downhill from the oak tree, on her own side of the burn. She came into full view and plodded to her mound, where she scratched herself, without suspicion, before going to ground. After her, from upstream, also on her own side, came Caileag. She sat down, below Coll, in front of her tunnel, clawed her neck, and went below. Keely, easily and instantly recognisable, returned soon after her and disappeared into the same tunnel. That left Bodach.

The sun was coming up, and the horizon cloudbank turned cinnamon, glowing to purple. The wind began to drop. A robin's waking trill made Coll think of raindrops; the waukrife hoodies cawed on their perches and shook their wings. Bodach's white face appeared on the up-slope and Coll watched him closely as he padded down the trail. At Coll's crossing place he stopped to sniff right and left, long and critically. Then, instead of running back in a panic, or bounding homewards, he turned left from the trail, and came shuffling towards the oak tree.

'Good God!' Coll said to himself under his breath.

Astonished and incredulous, but forced to believe what his eyes were seeing, he looked down at the badger and saw him rearing against the oak trunk, sniffing as high as he could reach. Then Bodach started to climb, clasping the trunk with his forepaws like a bear and digging in his claws. *This can't be happening*, Coll thought to himself. *The bliddy beast must be daft or seeking the deer fat!*

How far would the badger climb? Coll had no intention of waiting to find out, and maybe frightening the beast out of its wits. He had to startle it enough to turn it back without betraying himself, for it obviously had no idea he was there. But how?

All he could think of was matches, and he had a box of them in his side pocket. Quickly and quietly he took out the box, found a match, and rubbed the red head of it against the rough sandpaper edge. The scratch of it stopped Bodach when he was four feet from the ground, alerting him and puzzling him, but not yet alarming him. At the second scratch the match burst into flame, and that sent him down and away, and he was underground before Coll had blown it out.

Whew. Coll let out his breath. 'Who would ever have thocht to see the like o that?' The question was spoken; not a thought forming words in his head. He waited on for a few minutes in case the badger would look out again, then climbed down from the tree.

With all the badgers underground there was no more need for caution and none at all for haste. Coll massaged his fingertips, lit his pipe, and sat down under the tree to pull off his over-stockings, noting that the tobacco smoke was drifting along the frontage of the sett. He sniffed the stockings, flyped them, and stuffed them in his poacher's pocket. With his circulation restored he rose and left, side-footing and heeling his way down to the Breac, which he crossed by the badgers' stepping stones. From there he followed their trail to the Drochaid ride, then cut across the inbye to the farm, where he had left the Land Rover.

At seven o'clock in the morning, after a short sleep on the sofa and with oatcakes and cheese inside him, washed down with tea like tar, he was letting his poultry out when Simon appeared from the bothy.

'Good morning, Simon,' Coll greeted him.

'Guid mornin, Coll. I've a message for you.'

'At this time of the morning?'

'Aye. I was at a bit ceilidh last night, an this chap was tellin me there's a badger killt his hens. Well, his wife's seemingly the wan that says it. The man thinks it was a fox, but the wife'll no hae it onything but a badger. He was askin if you could maybe tak a look up and see what you think. Advise him like.'

'D'you ken the man?'

'No. Just met him last night. Name o MacRae.'

Coll thought for a moment. 'Canny say I ken him,' he said. 'How far is this place?'

'Six or seven miles up the road, then awa oot tae the left. It's an auld place it seems, no big, an kinofa broken doon they say.'

'You said I would come?'

'Well, I said you'd likely.'

'Then I'll go. In fact we'll both go.'

'Grand. The man'll be grand pleased. And noo that I get time to ask: hoo mony badgers did ye see?'

The half-frown left Coll's face. 'The lot cam back,' he said. 'And by cricks it was something. You should've seen it.'

'You should hae sent me a postcard. Wish you were here . . .'

'That'll be right. But dammit, man, there was one cam and climbed the tree I was up in! The same tree you were in, Simon. By cricks, thae beasts can climb! I had to fricht it away with a match or it would've been up in my lap . . .'

'Haud on there!' Simon said. 'It was me was at the *Ceilidh* daein the drammin.'

'Sure as daith,' Coll laughed. 'I kent the beasts would be in close ahint me at that time o the morning, and I had to cross one o their runs, so a beast coming in would be sure to get the scent of me and maybe go ram-stamming away. So not wanting to fricht it, I had an auld pair o stocking on ower my boots, slaigert wi deer fat, thinking maybe that would smother my scent. And, cricks, if this beast didn't run my line and start to climb the tree!'

'Jesus!' Simon said. 'And the match thing?'

'Well, you ken what good ears they've got, and I scarted a match thinking the noise would scare it away, and likely it would have, but the damned match caught fire. That frichted it away all right! But I'm sure it didn't know I was there.'

'An you think it was maybe the deer fat it was after?'

'It looked like it to me, but there could be some ither explanation.'

'Like maybe it just wanted tae scratch against the tree?'

'There's not a scratch on that oak, Simon. Anyway, they've got a tree they claw on, worn doon to a wasp waist. But if we're to see this chap of yours today we'd better get yokit. We'll be at the stags tomorrow.'

111

In ten minutes they reached the MacRae road-end, and Coll turned the Land Rover on to it. It was a rough track of whin metal and scalpings, rutted and pot-holed, with cross furrows worn out by running water. The verges were thistles and knapweed, scabious and harebell. The thistle heads were like moulting deer hair, and the downy seeds were drifting like mosquitoes across the road. A buzzard, perched on a telephone pole, stayed there, ignoring the Land Rover. Near the road a dead ewe was lying, eyeless and not fresh. Presently the men saw cattle and sheep on the hill, and soon the steading was in sight.

The steading, long neglected, was in a dilapidated state, and looked as though it might fall in on top of itself at any time. A man opened the gate into the closs when he saw the Land Rover approaching and closed it when Coll had driven through. He was a short man, broad as a door, with caliper legs, a clipped moustache, and eyes with a laugh in them. He shook hands with Coll.

'It was an imposeetion asking you to come,' he said. 'You'll have enough of your own to do without me wasting your time. But the missus'll hear of nothing but a badger.'

'It's no trouble,' Coll assured him. 'I don't know what we can do to help, but we'll try.'

The MacRae took them round the back of the steading to the henhouse. It was a rickety structure, with no floor, a leaky roof, and sagging sides – more like a Mrs Hen and wicked fox children's cartoon than a poultry cabin. A short length of board at the pop-hole end had been torn out. All round the henhouse was mud, hardly filmed by the frost of the night before, and on the mud were fox tracks as thick as brown flies on a dung pat. Coll and Simon walked round the henhouse, looking at the neat prints, then came back to where the board had been torn off. Coll knelt down and picked some red hair from the bottom of the lowest board. And at that moment MacRae's wife appeared.

She was a plump woman, with a stern face, and no laughter in her eyes. 'It was a badger,' she said. 'Nae doot aboot it! Durty brits!'

'This is Mr MacDonal from Dalnabreac,' McRae introduced

her. 'And his assistant, Mr Fraser. I tellt you I had asked him to come.'

She said: 'Oh!' and stood with arms akimbo. Coll offered her his hand but she ignored it.

'Durty brits,' she said again. 'Shouldny be encouraged.'

'It was a fox killed your hens, mistress,' Coll assured her. 'There's only fox tracks here, and . . .'

'I dinny care aboot tracks,' she interrupted him. 'It was a badger took them.' She looked defiantly at Coll. 'And naebody'll make me chinge my mind.'

'But look, mistress, there's no badger tracks here at all,' Coll said. 'And there's this fox hair I took from . . .'

'I'm no bothered aboot tracks or hair,' she interrupted him again. 'It was a badger took them. I'm the wan that lost them, so I should ken!'

'A red badger wearin fox boots,' Simon said with mock gravity.

'Don't get funny wi me, buster,' she snapped at him. 'An uncle o mine was a keeper in Argyll. An he learned me aboot badgers.'

'But look Agnes,' MacRae tried to reason with her. 'These chaps ken what they're talking about. Will you listen?'

'An I ken what I'm talkin aboot tae,' she flared at him.

'It's like this, mistress,' Coll tried again. 'A badger couldn't come here without leaving its tracks. And there's not a . . .'

'It was a badger,' she insisted. 'Durty brits.' And she went back into the house.

'I'm sorry about that, Mr MacDonald,' MacRae apologised. 'But you can see the state she's in.'

'That's all right,' said Coll. 'I'm sorry too. But we tried.'

'You wouldn't care for a bit dram before you go?' MacRae offered.

'Some other time maybe, but thank you all the same,' Coll said.

All he wanted was to be away: to hell out of it as he said later. On the drive home he asked Simon: 'Well, what did you think of that?'

113

'A colt revolver, that one,' Simon said. 'Six words maximum an every wan a man deid!'

Coll shook his head. 'How can any man put up with the like of that?'

'What surprises me,' said Simon, 'is the way you managed to keep your temper wi her.'

'My temper,' said Coll in a quiet voice, 'is like my prejudices. 'I don't part with it readily.'

Chapter Ten

Many fine stags were grassed on Dalnabreac that season, including two Royals and a hummel. A Royal is a mature hart with twelve points on his antlers – brow, bay and tray tines, with three-point top forming a cup: a hummel has no antlers at all. Stags have to be killed whether they carry trophy heads or not; but trophies are what those who kill them usually want. Nobody wants hummels and taking them out, like taking out hinds, is stalkers' work. Coll was parsimonious with the best heads, ensuring sustained yield, which is jargon for leaving some alive to breed more. He succeeded in persuading a Cavalry Club major to forego a thirteen-pointer because next season the beast might become an Imperial.

The badgers were not affected by the stalking: like grouse shooting it was a daytime activity. Even Bodach, lying at the entrance to his tunnel on sunny mornings, heard nothing of it, for the rifle fire was far away, beyond the Piper's Cairn and round Ben Dearg. But the daytime hunters knew about it, and some of them stalked the stalkers, for when a stag is killed he is gralloched where he falls and his paunch and entrails left for the scavengers of the hill – the ravens, hoodies, buzzards, jackdaws and foxes.

It was into the rut – the days of roaring – before the badgers became aware again of the red deer, for they had summered high on Ben Dearg, in hind groups and stag groups, segregated. Now, with their new antlers cleaned of the velvet, the big stags were warming to the rut, and in ones and twos were leaving their fellows and breaking into the hind grounds, heralding their arrival with leonine roars.

They came striding down from the high ground – maned, swollen of neck, fired with the fever of the rut – to wallow in peat hags and emerge, clarted and dripping like primeval monsters, while Orion glittered and the Aurora flickered with blue and amethyst flames. They ripped grass and heather with their antlers and the nights were filled with their roaring. They rushed this way and that, vapouring, gathering hinds, and the smell of them was heavy on the air.

Twenty-three hinds with fifteen calves were rounded up by a big switch-horn stag with grey face and leonine mane, and herded near the Piper's Cairn. All night he chivvied and circled them, drinking much from saps and puddles and eating not at all; running here and there and yonder; challenging, driving off lesser beasts trying to raid his harem, and always roaring. The hinds behaved casually, allowing him to herd them; but they were cool, even indifferent, and grazed and rested while he challenged and postured and wore himself out to hold them. Five lesser stags were skirmishing around his harem, but only when one intruded within his toleration distance did he leave the hinds to chase him. Unlike the roebuck, the red stag holds hinds, not ground.

Bodach crossed the grass moor one night when Ben Dearg, crowned with the first grizzle of snow, glowed purple against a Valkyriean sky and the pools on the Slainte levels were plated with fire. He could hear the big switch roaring, and his nose wrinkled on the smell of him before he saw the dark shapes of deer crowded across the trail ahead. Bodach padded on at a slow, inswinging trot, with no thought of detouring from his own well trodden path, and the alert deer saw the white face of him approaching. Hinds on their feet stood aside for him; those lying down rose to look at him; the switch lowered his head and grunted but made no threatening move.

For part of the night Bodach hunted the grassland, keeping well below the switch and his hinds, and found five dead voles. He also caught one alive. Then the Drochaid magnetism drew him again and he crossed the bridge of planks into The Corrach, where he found Mathair bellied down under the branches of a windfall eating a rabbit. It was a big rabbit, beyond her usual ability to run down and catch, but it was slow-witted, recovering from myxomatosis, and she had been able to surprise it and kill it without a chase. She held it down firmly with her forepaws when she saw Bodach, and growled at him when he tried to sniff it. He left her with it and went on to Ash Tree, where he slept for two hours before setting out for Drochaid. In the kitchen garden he dug up and ate a carrot, then went brambling along the hedgerows for the rest of the night.

On most nights, after dusk or in the hours before dawn, he visited the grass moor. Although the vole numbers were dwindling, he could still find dead ones, and catch enough of them alive to make hunting them worthwhile. The big switch was still there with his harem, but not always in the same place, for if the senior hind decided to change ground he had to follow or lose them. He could herd them and hold them, but not on ground where she did not want to be. On the tenth night of his overlordship he was blown and lean, with tucked-up belly; and on that night Bodach was lying dozing in the rock cleft below the Piper's Cairn.

The moon was up in a clear sky when a tall ten-pointer stag strode on to the switch's ground, roaring in challenge: he was strong, grushie and newly come to the rut. At once the switch ran to meet him. The ten-pointer halted, with hindlegs braced, presenting a bold front. They roared and grunted at each other, with antlers lowered; but there was no head-on clash. The newcomer side-stepped, seeking a flank, and the switch moved sideways to keep him in front. They touched antlers and side-stepped again. For twenty yards they moved, sideways to the left, not engaging; then sideways to the right, still not engaging. Then the ten-pointer put down his head and charged.

Taken by surprise, or perhaps because he was worn out (run-out is the way they say it on the deer forest) the switch was thrust back – back – back – slotting and furrowing the peat. He was pushed on to his haunches; he was prodded in the flank; he was hustled into a dub of water. When he struggled to his feet, dripping sludge, there was no more fight in him. He turned away and trotted, high-kneed and spring-footed, from the ground. For him the days and nights of roaring were over. The hinds accepted the new master as indifferently as they had accepted the old.

During the rut Bodach began to change his routine, visiting the grass moor and The Corrach less frequently, and spending more of each night in the glen or at Drochaid, visiting the farm when everyone was abed and the collie Nell asleep in the hayshed. Having been in the kitchen garden once, and eaten a carrot, which he liked, he began to make a habit of visiting it, digging up no more than one root on a night. Suddenly, there were no more carrots, for Drummond had harvested them and stored them in boxes of sand in an outhouse. But there were still brussels sprouts and parsnips. He dug up a fat-bellied, thin-tailed parsnip from which he took only one bite. The sprouts seemed to have more appeal to him, and he ate two.

Drummond knew he had a visitor, and his mind was on rabbits or a hare until Coll pointed badger tracks out to him, when he laughed uproariously and said: 'What the hell! Wan sprout or parsnip whiles is neethur here nor there. As the man said: *a daimen icker in a thrave's a sma request.*' He was a great man for quoting Burns, not misquoting, and could read and speak Scots as well as he could read and speak English, and that forbye his native Gaelic. For he was a Gael born and bred, and a gey haun at the pibroch, as they said.

Round the outside of the kitchen garden the fence was happed with dogwood and blackthorn, hawthorn and snow-berry, cotoneaster and guelder rose, and on each corner there was a pear tree, heavy with fruit. Bodach ate none of the berries. But Drummond collected the grape-like fruits of the black-thorn, which he called slae, and made them up with gin – the same sloe gin they make in the English west country.

When the stag season was over, and the stalkers had begun the routine killing of hinds, the badgers harvested acorns and beech mast, eating them as they fell and sometimes in quantity. Less frequently they lifted and nibbled at the propeller seeds of field maple and sycamore, and the bunched keys of the ash. Jays were also gathering acorns, gobbling some and burying others against the lean days ahead. Some of them the birds would find again; others they would forget about. The forgotten acorns would sprout into seedlings, and some would even grow on to become trees; but most would be eaten to the ground by rabbits and deer, and the few that recovered would grow stunted. None of the Breac badgers buried food; their store was the fat on their bodies.

Woodmice were foraging in the hazels on the burnside flats, ferrying nuts away for storage or gnawing through the shells to eat the kernels; unripe nuts, still clasped in green, they nibbled at perfunctorily or left alone. Bank voles were also feeding on nuts, gnawing into the kernel in the same way; but unlike the woodmice they left no tooth marks on the shells. Keely was the first of the badger clan to exploit the nut harvest; next morning, in good light, she was joined by Bodach, then Mathair and Caileag, and lastly by Caileag's cubs. That morning six badgers went to ground. Mathair's cubs were back at Ash Tree.

The badgers gathered nuts as far as they could reach, after snapping up those lying on the ground. They took them green or ripe, crushing them with their back teeth, grinding and swallowing most of the shells, but ejecting sharp, curved slivers from the sides of their mouths. The slivers resembled nothing that had ever been touched by the teeth of woodmice, voles or squirrels.

Despite the richness of the seed harvest the badgers did not desert the Drochaid fields and hedgerows, and on lown nights, after rain, Bodach went there first to hunt surfacing earthworms and snap up others drowning, or dead, in puddles and flood-water. On some nights he gorged on them, taking no other food; on others he bulked out the worms with pig-nuts dug from hedgebottoms. Drummond was now recognising the badger scrapes – which he had once thought were the work of rabbits – so was not surprised when he found one, half filled with soft dung, on the cornfield endrigg. In the field he had twenty-four weaned calves, grazing the foggage, for he liked new grass eaten down in the autumn. When the calves were taken off it would grow on to become next summer's hay – untouched between times by any other mouths.

The calves were strong, black and hornless – well fleshed hallanshakers fidging for the ploy. When they saw Bodach entering the field from a gap in the hedgerow they crowded in on him, with their heads down and their tails in the air. They pounded after him in a body. He *woofed* at them in annoyance, and they backed away for the space of six snorts while he creamed the green from a fresh dung pat with his tongue. Then they followed him again, almost treading on his scut – in phalanx behind with skirmishers on his flanks – and forced him under the fence into the rootfield, where sixty cross-Blackface hoggs were folded on the swedes.

The sheep had eaten off the shaws, and the field was polka-dotted with topless turnips bitten into the white pulp. The smell of sheep was heavy on the air – a brooding cloud of warm breath and body smell, unexciting to Bodach. He had no interest in sheep. But they were unsure of him, if not alarmed. They broke away down the drills for a short distance – jostling, shouldering, stotting, mounting one another – then faced about, milling in a bourach: some snorting, some stamping, and all watching the badger. Still unexcited, Bodach bit a piece from a swede, munched it and swallowed it. He bit off and ate a second piece before turning away from the sheep and into the inbye, where two Highland ponies were munching hay beside the new six-strand fence along the ride.

The ponies winded him before they saw the white arrowhead of him bobbing and weaving towards them. They dropped their wisps of hay, lowered their heads, kicked their shod hindfeet in the air, and walked out to meet him, nickering their awareness of him. Bodach, hearing them and seeing the sudden great bulk of them, halted to watch them; the ponies pulled up a few paces from him, with their weight forward, and studied him. They shook their heads and reached out to him with soft, questing muzzles – all curiosity, with ears up and no threat of hostility. Then, suddenly, they wheeled aside and thudded away at a gallop, with manes and tails flying.

Bodach padded to the fence and walked over their hay to their wooden feeding trough, from which he licked the last morsels of bruised oats. The trace-smell and -taste of treacle excited him and he sniffed along the trough seeking the source. He climbed over it, and walked in it, scraping with his teeth where he could smell the elusive treacle, and even swallowing cribbings that held the taste of it. Realising syne that the smell had no substance he gave up and followed the fence to the Drochaid kitchen garden, leaving his teeth scrapes for the ponyman to puzzle over in the morning.

On the first corner he found windfall pears, shaken from the tree by a gale during the day. He gathered a pear in his forepaws, squirrel-like, bit into it with his side teeth, and quickly cut it in two. Liking the taste, he ate both pieces, crunching them with his back teeth. The flesh was hard but sweet, and the juice pleasing to his palate. He cut up and ate three more pears, by which time his stomach was gorged. Before leaving he raked a few pears together and clawed tufts of withered grass and leaves lightly over them. He carried none away.

After two nights of frost, followed by a morning of ermine cranreuch, the iron was in the ground, and Drummond moved his calves from the foggage to the cattle reed, where he would over-winter them, feeding them on home grown hay and oats. Next day he was on the cropped foggage with the dung spreader, and by nightfall a third of the field was brown and laned with tyre tracks but not rutted. Soon after the machine had finished for the day Bodach arrived in the field, with Mathair following a little way behind – both attracted by the wind-borne tidings of freshly spread, well rotted farmyard muck, in which earthworms might be found.

Experience had taught Bodach that earthworms could be found in the wake of the dung spreader, celled in the lumps or lurking in the touzles. Tonight there would still be worms in the dung, or dead on the frozen ground into which they could not escape. For two hours the badgers hunted the area, separately but not far apart, running this way and that, turning over strawy bits and pieces and shaking out the big clods with their claws. The worms they caught were mostly small – a special breed unlike the soil monsters of grassland and arable – but to a badger a worm is a worm, whatever its size or life style.

Bodach left the field before Mathair and made his way to the farm dung midden, treading warily, with ears and nose alert, in case Nell was loose. She was not. She was in the kitchen, where Drummond often allowed her, being a non-believer in the canon that a working dog should be kept out of the house. Bodach mounted the disturbed dungheap in the midden, clawed and scraped in the unfrozen surface, and caught a few more worms. By the time he had eaten all he could find his white face was clarted brown and green, and he smelled not like a badger; but he cleaned his feet, face and coat afterwards by clawing and rolling in frosted tussocks. Before leaving for home he visited the kitchen midden where he poked his face into a syrup tin seeking with his tongue the last honey-sweet dregs.

Next day was Sunday and Coll and Simon were walking in the glen with a teacher from the village school and twelve of her pupils. The children had chosen badgers for a project at school, and Coll had promised to take them on a nature walk, which had to be on a Sunday because he was busy with the hinds and it was his only free day of the week. The children were well shod and well wrapped, and not two of them dressed alike. Miss Lindsay, the teacher, was trewed in Lindsay tartan. Tarf the terrier was running through the group, wagging her tail and fussing, and being patted and fussed in return.

It was a crisp, cloudless sunny morning of silvered grass and grizzled trees, with cats' whiskers of gossamer in the hazels, and two jet fighters crossing vapour trails to make a saltire in the blue arach of sky above Ben Dearg. On the trail to the badger sett Coll pointed out siskins, goldcrests, bullfinches, jays, a heron, and blackcocks in ebony buskins gobbling cones in the alders beside the Breac. The children were excited and talkative, and Coll said:

'Quiet now! The way not to see anything is to chatter like magpies.'

'That's right,' Simon warned from the rear. 'It's gettin like a bird cage at the zoo.' They thought that was funny, and some of them giggled, covering their mouths with a hand.

Although the stalkers were both telescope men they were that day carrying binoculars, and when they saw a buzzard wheeling above The Corrach they adjusted them so that all the children could look at it. At the Breac stepping stones Coll asked them all to sit down while he talked to them. Two girls sat with Tarf, fussing her, and laughed when she licked their faces.

'She'll put up wi plenty o that,' he told them.

'She's very gentle for a working terrier, isn't she?' Miss Lindsay asked.

'Seems to me they're a bit like folks,' Coll answered her. 'The real hard cases are generally quiet and weel mannert. Now,' he turned to the youngsters, 'you see these stepping stones? Well, they're used by the badgers on their way home from this side of the burn. That's the sett over there, up the hill a bitty, like a row o big moudie heaps. I'll take you across to see it syne, but first maybe you'd like to ask something?'

They were slow to respond, so he went on: 'There's a family in the sett. They eat just about anything they can catch, but fruit and the like as well, and they're byornar fond of wasps and worms, and whiles they'll tak a bit venison in the winter if they come across a dead deer.'

A tall girl, with Titian hair and a tasselled bonnet, said:

'Please sir, Hamish Campbell says . . .' She stopped, shyly, putting her hand over her mouth. Coll looked a question at Miss Lindsay.

'He's the keeper's boy . . . you know? . . . But not here . . .'

'And what does Hamish Campbell say?' Coll smiled gently.

'He says his father says badgers are dirty brutes . . . and they kill lambs . . . Hamish says . . .'

'Well,' Coll said gravely, 'the badgers here don't. You can ask Pharic the shepherd.'

'Hamish Campbell says too . . .' the girl put her hand over her mouth, and giggled. 'He says his father kills them . . .'

'I wonder why,' Coll said. 'But I suppose Hamish's father will ken his ain business best.'

A red-headed boy with a fernitickled face put up his hand and said to the girl, almost like a declaration of war: 'I ken why he kills badgers. He gets them made into sporrans!'

Coll looked at the teacher. Then he said to the children: 'Don't you think that the best place for a badger's skin to be is on a badger where it belongs?'

'Yes, sir!' they answered in chorus.

'Please sir,' the girl with the Titian hair put up her hand again. 'Hamish Campbell says his father says . . .'

'I think,' Coll interrupted her as gently as he knew how, 'that we should forget about Hamish and his sayings now. Don't you?'

'Sir?' asked he with the carrot head and the fernitickles. 'Can you show us a fox den as well?'

'Now? No! Foxes are in the one place for only a short time of the year, when the vixens have cubs. The rest of the time they're oot ower a. But badgers are thirled to the one place all the time, and that's why they're so much easier to kill than foxes – for folks that want to kill them, that is.'

'Why do you kill deer?' a grave-faced little boy asked. He had a dark sheemach head and blue eyes with a dream in them.

'Well,' Coll said, reading the boy's thoughts, 'we once had wolves and wolves killed deer, and people also killed them to eat them. Now we have no wolves and we have to kill deer even if

124

people didn't want to eat them. If we didn't, they'd be all over Scotland, and maybe we'd all have to flit to make room for them. The eagles take a few calves but that's not enough. So Mr Fraser and I have to kill a certain number every year, but we pick the ones to be killed and do the best we can.'

'Thank you,' the boy said.

'Look!' Coll exclaimed suddenly pointing out to Ben Dearg. 'Take these!' he said to the girl beside him, handing her his binoculars. 'Look there! Can you see them?'

'Yes,' the girl said. 'What are they?'

'The eagles. Three of them. The pair and the young one.'

Everybody became excited, and two pairs of binoculars passed from hand to hand. The children all saw the birds before they disappeared behind Ben Dearg.

'Fancy that!' Miss Lindsay said to the youngsters. 'Three eagles. Isn't that a bonus?'

'Yes, miss,' they said in chorus.

'Now then,' Coll said to them. 'Let's to the badger sett. How many of you can cross by the stones? But, hold on a minute.' He tied Tarf to a tree and told her to wheesht. 'How many of you want carried across?'

'Why are you tying up the dog?' asked the girl with the Titian hair.

'Because I don't want her near the badgers. She's been cut up once already.'

'By badgers?'

'By a badger. When I made the mistake of letting her go in after a fox that was there, and thinking the badger wasn't when it was.'

The two men carried four girls across the Breac. Simon misjudged a step when he was carrying his second and filled his braw veldtschoen boots with water.

'I'm sorry about that,' Miss Lindsay said.

'That's all right,' Simon laughed. 'Once they're wet they're wet, and canna get ony wetter, and after that you don't bother.' He carried a third girl across without even trying to find shallow footing.

Coll took the party in file along the frontage of the sett, with Simon bringing up the rear. He pointed out the holes, filled with leaves, that were not in use, and the well padded entrances that were. He showed them the five-clawed tracks of the badgers and their scratching post. Then he took them all uphill and down wind, where they gathered round him with more questions.

'I don't want too much of our scent lying about,' he told them, 'although it should be maistly gone by the time the beasts come out after dark.'

'I'd like to see the badgers,' the girl with the Titian hair said.

'So would I,' said carrot head. 'Could we?'

'Yes,' said Coll. 'But it'll have to be after February month, when we're finished with the hinds. And that's a good time too.'

'Would you?' Miss Lindsay asked.

'Yes, of course,' Coll said. 'I'm grand pleased they're keen enough to want to. Just keep me minded nearer the time.'

'Thank you.'

'By here!' Simon laughed. 'You fairly walked into that wi your een wide shut. You'll hae tae tape their mooths an nail them tae a tree!'

Coll said to Miss Lindsay: 'I wonder if you chaps would mind if I dinna come back with you? I'd like tae gang on the hill a bitty to spy the hinds for tomorrow.'

'Not at all,' she said. 'Can we get back from this side?'

'Haud on there,' said Simon. 'I'm gaun back wi ye, remember? Somebody has to drive the Land Rover.'

'Of course,' Coll shook his head. 'I must be getting doitit. Miss Lindsay has her car. Well, you chaps,' he said to the children, 'safe home and *beannachd leibh*.'

The girl with the Titian hair came over to him, shook his hand, and said: 'Goodbye to you, and thank you – *gu'n robh math agaibh*.' The others shook hands with him and thanked him. Carrot head said: 'That was grand, sir. Will I go and bring your wee dug across?'

'No,' said Coll, 'but thanks just the same. I'm going out on that side.'

Chapter Eleven

Coll followed The Corrach trail, not hurrying, with Tarf trotting behind or at his side. The air was still in the pinewood and he soon began to feel warm. Here and there along the trail he saw hand-footed badger tracks hardened by frost, like plaster casts, but there was no scent in them. The tracks meant nothing to Tarf: she could smell, not read, sign. Her eyes were her nose, and there was nothing for it to own.

Sealgair the tawny owl, roosting in a pine tree beside the trail, drawn-up tall and wizened against the trunk, opened a dark, lustrous eye when he heard the man's footsteps below. When the footsteps stopped he shrank shorter, filled out to owl-shape, and stared down with both eyes wide, swaying on his perch. He saw the man looking up and the terrier casting about the base of the tree. Side-stepping away from the trunk he danced on his perch, stretched his neck, shook his head, and from his cleft mouth bocked up a wet pellet, which Tarf pounced on when it hit the ground. She sniffed it over, wrinkled her nose, then left it at Coll's low-voiced: 'Come oot o that!'

Two blackbirds came to chivvy the owl the moment man and dog had gone, and Coll could hear the *pinking* of them all the way to Ash Tree fork. *Owl talk*, he thought to himself. A man could always depend on the blackbirds to betray an owl stirring or disturbed.

He turned off at the fork and walked to Ash Tree sett, with some idea in his head about teaching Tarf what not to do about badger holes; despite her mauling she was still too reckless, still too eager to go to ground without first asking questions with her nose. Near the sett, but not too near, was a rimed pine stump. He sat down on it and lit his pipe, keeping Tarf at his feet, with his hand lightly stroking her rump. She knew the sett was there, and was trembling with excitement, tempted to break but resisting it, knowing the meaning of the hand on her rump.

'Ware badger, Tarf!' Coll kept whispering to her, gently stern. 'Leave it now! Leave it!'

Patience was a recessive gene in Tarf's make-up, and Coll knew how sorely she was being tried; but she had to learn, and this was one way of teaching her without blunting her cutting edge. Each time she tried to inch away from his feet he spoke to her:

'Ware badger! Leave it now. Leave it!'

He smoked on, watching her closely, holding her by voice and hand stroke, and at last she lay down beside him, with her tongue quivering over her teeth, looking up at him and around, with her tail wagging, as though badgers were the last thing in her head. Coll rose, warning her to stay where she was, and walked to the nearest entrance to the sett. He knelt beside it and looked into it. When she half rose to come on he put up his hand and warned her: 'Ware badger! Leave it!' She sat down again, whimpering through closed teeth, with a low grumble in her chest.

Coll rose smartly and walked back to her. 'Good girl,' he fussed her. 'Come on now! To heel!' She looked longingly at the badger holes but she followed him, dancing at his heels and leaping to his hand all the way back to the fork.

Goldcrests were flitting like bumblebees in The Corrach pines. On a high branch a red squirrel was sitting shredding a cone, and when Coll swung the glass from it he picked up a hen capercaillie in the next tree pulling and eating pine shoots. He left The Corrach by the bridge of planks over the Breac and headed for the Piper's Cairn. On the grassland a short-eared owl was hunting – slow-flapping, rising, dipping and gliding. Coll smiled when Tarf pounced on a vole, chopped it and swallowed it; but when she put up a mountain hare, patchy white in the moult, he ordered her from the chase: 'Leave it!' She came back with her tail down. 'That's good,' he said to her, and her tail came up again.

From the Piper's Cairn he spied along the Slainte and up to Ben Dearg. On a pool two goosanders were swimming and splashing. Farther upstream an otter was diving and surfacing, and rolling on to its back in play. It left the pool, ran hump-backed along the shore, dived back into the water, and surfaced on to a boulder where it sat tall in weasel pose – a sheened figurine in the slanting sun. It was a dog otter. Presently three other otters appeared on the pool, trailing their V-wakes to-wards the boulder. The dog otter snake-glided into the water to join them, and Coll watched the four of them playing until they disappeared from view under the near bank. *Well, well, well* he said to himself, and slapped the telescope shut.

From the shoulder of Ben Dearg, above the heather line, he spied three parcels of hinds in hollows, grazing at a slow walk, and he reckoned they would not move far before morning. He sat on for a while watching them and smoking his pipe, with Tarf lying at his feet. Grouse were crowing in the heather. Coll put the glass up again and spied the place where he had gralloched a hind the day before. The ravens Pruk and Borb were feeding on it, with five hoodie crows standing by waiting their turn. Before he put away the glass he spied up to the grizzled crown of Ben Dearg, in time to see Iolair the eagle swinging down, banking and flying to his roosting ledge.

Instead of taking the direct route back to The Corrach footbridge, he made a wide detour and followed the Slainte, hoping he might see the otters again. There was no sign of them near the pool except a spraint, which Tarf quickly found and examined with her nose. By the time they reached the bridge the sun was a crimson fireball in a furnace of clouds, with a pallid egg-shaped moon, far behind, trailing it across the sky. Soon it would be badger light, and an idea began to take shape in Coll's head.

He was nearing Ash Tree fork when the idea became a decision. He would wait on, with Tarf on a cord, to see how she would react to the smell and sight of the Ash Tree badgers on foot. The sett might not be occupied but he was prepared to wait for an hour or so to find out. A little way downhill was a big pine against which he could stand, with his shape concealed from the badgers and his scent out of their noses. Tarf came to him at his whispered command, and it was then he saw a badger coming towards him, on the main trail from the Breac, its white face nodding and clearly visible at forty yards. The badger was Bodach, and Mathair and Caileag were not far behind.

The badger had the wind, what little there was of it, at his back, so Coll knew he would not be smelling man or dog, and at the distance he would certainly not be seeing them. It was equally certain that Tarf would presently wind the badger, and within seconds she would see him. Coll reached down to lift her. The badger came steadily on. Then Tarf broke away . . .

But not towards the badger. She broke downhill, crashing in the frush ground cover, and not barking. Coll took his eyes from the trail for a moment, and when he looked back the badger was no longer there. Where had it gone? Up, down, or back? There was crashing below the place where the beast had been, a noise too great for a small terrier to make. So it had to be the badger. But why had the beast left the trail? And if Tarf was chasing it why had she rushed downhill instead of running upwind straight to it? Coll was puzzled. *There's a thing wrong*, he thought to himself, and went leaping, sclaffing and sliding down after the terrier.

And there was a sight for any man's eyes to disbelieve, or as Coll was to say later: a sight a man couldn't dream up with twenty-six and two thirds fluid ounces of a hundred and four proof straight malt inside him. In a pool, between steep rocky banks, crowded over with alders, the ten-pointer stag from the

130

Piper's Cairn was plunging and swinging his head, stumbling and rearing, with a terrier on the end of his nose.

Tarf . . .

'Christ Almighty!' Coll exclaimed. 'You stupid little bugger of a dog!' But there was more anguish than anger in the words. 'Tarf! Tarf! Leave it, d'ye hear? Leave it, dog, for God's sake.'

The stag threw up his head, trying to toss the terrier clear; he lowered it and dipped her in the pool. She gurgled and snorted but kept her grip. He half turned, and Coll reached out with the crook of his stick, trying to catch Tarf by the neck. He missed. The stag dipped her again, tossed his head high trying to throw her, and Coll expected to see her flying through the air at any moment. But she held on. 'You thrawn bitch!' Coll shouted at her in anguished concern. Then the stag did what he was afraid he would try.

He lowered his head and stabbed through the screen of alders to the steep rocky bank. He made contact with his top tines, not his face, and that left the terrier hanging short, in a web of alder twigs. The stag kept boring at the rock, and shaking his head, trying to take her on a brow fork. But he failed to crush her or dirk her. Coll clouted him on the head with his stick, a futile reflex action, for the stag could not let go of the dog. When he drew back from the alder screen, and plunged in the pool again, Coll reached out and clouted Tarf with the stick. But she would not release her hold, and there was no way Coll could help her, without running the risk of being thrown or tossed, and gored in half a dozen places.

In the end she was saved by near-drowning. The next time the stag dipped her he stumbled and fell on his face, submerging her for a few seconds. Tarf released her grip and surfaced, coughing and gasping for air, as he was scrambling back to his feet. She saw him and paddled towards him, trying to leap at him from the water, but he did not wait for her. Realising he was free of her he splashed downstream from the pool, coughing; then he was out on to the bank and away uphill at a gallop, with his head high and his nose dripping blood.

131

Tarf swam ashore and shook herself, still coughing and spluttering. Instead of waiting for Coll to come to her, or running to him, she bolted uphill. But she did not go far. When he caught up with her she was sitting at a hole under an outcrop of rock, panting, with her tongue out at full stretch, and wagging her tail.

'For pity's sake, dog, what now?' he asked her.

She rose, sniffed at the hole, looked at him, and reared against his knees, scratching with her forepaws. When he knelt by the hole she licked his face. Coll looked into it and could see nothing; the light from the brightening moon was not reaching it. He struck a match and held it, wavering, at the dark entrance. In its flame, five feet ben, he saw the rump of a badger. The beast was digging – away from the entrance! The badger was Bodach . . .

Coll sat down and took Tarf in his lap. He felt over her ribs, her back and her legs, without bringing a yelp from her. Remarkably, she was unhurt.

'Well, by cricks!' he said to her. 'You've had a gey day the day, and now you think you're back in the good books because you've turned up your nose at badger.'

Tarf was shivering. He patted her, called her to heel, and started off on the badger trail to Drochaid, walking at a brisk pace to help her warm up. They were above the Breac stepping stones when he saw two badgers coming on the up trail from the burn. He stopped, and waved Tarf down. Mathair and Caileag bolted back to the stepping stones, then face about, arcing their noses in query. Coll whispered Tarf to heel, and walked on as quietly as he could.

In the bothy, over a dram, he told Simon about the rest of his day. Simon looked at Tarf and took her on his knee.

'By God, dog, you're a sowpit!' he said.

'What took her to the stag,' Coll said, 'God alone knows. And dammit, she kent where the badger was as well. She showed me, and damn the girn did she greet.'

'You're damned lucky, dog, the stag didna fork ye up like a sausage,' Simon told her.

132

'You ken, Simon, I fairly thocht it was curtains for her,' Coll said in a serious voice.

Simon ran his hand along her back, and said: 'I dinna ken hoo many lives a dog has, but this wan's sure workin on overdraft!'

The egg-shaped moon was far down the sky, flooding the Ash Tree trail with light, when Bodach left the hole under the rock, after long testing with his nose to make sure that man and dog had gone. The night was windless, the frost hardening, and the pine needles silvering. The rusty ferns were grey as a badger's back thatch, and every brushwood stick was rimed. The Breac was freezing over, and across the pool, where Tarf had fastened on to the nose of a stag, a water vole was scurrying, black in the moonlight, with stars in its eyes.

Bodach padded uphill, slowly and warily, to the trail, and stopped, sniffing at the ground and arcing his snout. Perhaps some trace scent of man and dog still lingered there, for he turned back downhill and walked to the pool, and there he stopped again. The water vole was no longer on the ice. Here too, perhaps, was nuance of man and dog smell from the pool to the trail, for again he turned about and followed the Breac upstream, with his mind on Drochaid. On the way he rooted in the leaf litter, grunting and champing his jaws, swallowing some of the withered leaves with whatever else he was finding in it.

In the Drochaid ride he wandered about among heaps of sand, road metal and drain pipes; round and under earth movers, dumper trucks and a cement mixer. He scrambled up and over a stack of roofing timber. He rubbed his rump against the base of a cement mixer, leaving some betraying hairs on it. Near one of the huts used by the workers he found a dustbin with a black rubber lid; the lid concealed the contents of the bin but not the exciting smell. He scooped off the lid, overturned the bin, and bored into it, scooping out the contents.

Before he left it – on its side, six feet from where it had stood – he had licked clean a tin labelled *Macaroni and Cheese*, another labelled *Tomato Soup*, and eaten cheese and bacon rind, two crusts of white bread, the core of an apple, and a small piece of foil that smelled of chocolate. The rubber lid seemed to fascinate him, and for reasons known only to himself he clawed it, upended it and rolled it, pulled it against his chest and backed off with it as though he were gathering bedding. It was fifteen yards from its starting point when he tired of it.

He prowled round the second hut, as though in search of more dustbins, and found none. Next he made a complete tour of the foundations of six cottages, where the first brick had yet to be laid, and found nothing except empty bottles and cans that had contained the worthless fizz-pop with which men like to test the stamina of their alimentary tracts. Inside one cottage foundation he tried to scrape a hole in the ground, but the frost defeated even his powerful bear claws. So he squatted on the concrete found and deposited his dung there: a lone miniscule cairn which, along with the peregrinating dustbin lid, sorely tried the detective skills of the men in the morning.

The centre of the ride was now a road, not yet finished, but rolled firm and flat and being used by motor cars. Bodach walked along the middle of it, his body a moving shadow on the dark road metal following the white arrowhead of his face. A heap of four-inch clay tiles on one side attracted him, and he clambered on to it, starting a miniature avalanche which he rode to the ground. The slide broke three tiles, chipped four and cracked two, which was trifling damage, not likely to change the colour of the ink on onybody's bank account. Bodach shambled away from the ruins, scuffed in a pad but not noticing it.

The next heap was of concrete pipes, big enough in diameter to admit the biggest badger, and he walked into one. It was roomier inside than the widest tunnel at the Breac sett. He rolled over in it, bellied down, bit and licked his pads, and clawed a flank with a hindfoot. It was a place he might well have chosen to lie up in, had he been ready to lie up. He was not. More than half the night was still ahead of him, and he had eaten little, so he had the urge to carry on hunting, despite the frost. When he rose to leave the pipe he found himself face to face with

Drummond's Nell – out rabbiting in the battlefield of the ride before going to bed for the night in the hayshed.

The sudden confrontation startled him. He became angry, and growled, showing her the tip of the arrow. Secure in his pipe, he was prepared to wait; and Nell, still callow, but remembering, had no thought of trying to draw him. She was young, she was curious, and she was vaunty – with time to spare for a ploy. She barked at him, chesting the ground and wagging her tail; she darted at him in mock threat, then leaped aside or back-tracked. She danced around, and reared, barking and baying to the sky. When she probed too close to the pipe she was met by an arrowhead clicking teeth. That was a warning she understood, and heeded. She lost interest in the pipe and trotted off home.

Drummond, late home with his wife from a barn dance, was putting away his car when she arrived in the closs. 'Where've you been stravaiging to at this time o night?' he greeted her sternly. She ran to his wife, who said: 'Don't come running to me for sympathy, my girl.' Nell skulked to the stable with her tail down, and waited. Drummond opened the door and put her in with the Highland ponies for the night. Locking her in the stable was his punishment when she had misdeemed, as he put it.

When Bodach left the pipe he prowled along the hedgerows, rooting in the bottoms and scraping in the frozen litter; then on to the big pasture, now unoccupied by cattle, where he turned over crusted dung pats. He visited the cornfield foggage but found no worms in the frozen dung. About an hour and a half before anyone was due to stir at the farm he was back there, behind the cattle reed, where he found a ten ton load of sand piled against the gable of the tractor shed, which was being re-roofed and repaired. In the sand heap was a hole, and the smell coming from it, mustily warm, was rat. He started to claw at the hole.

But the sand crust was frozen hard as rock, and at first his claws made as little impression on it as they would have made on concrete. He scraped, bit and grunted, dislodging only a few chips. The young beasts in the reed heard him, and a few of the more curious rose to look at him, snorting vapour and oil-cake breath to add to the frore. The farm tortoiseshell cat turned the corner of the tractor shed, saw him, and bolted; she had been at the hole earlier and was returning for another vigil. Bodach worked on, grunting and breathing noisily, unaware of the cat's visit and ignoring his audience of cattle.

At last he broke away the hard ring at the entrance to the rat-hole. He inserted a paw, exerted his full strength, and broke off a chunk the size of a walnut; he probed again with the paw, pulled, and broke off two more. That let him in with both sets of foreclaws and he scooped away bigger chunks; then he was into the soft sand, burrowing like a great mole, scraping the spoil out between his hindlegs. Within a few minutes he had the nest uncovered.

It was at the back of the heap, hard against the gable – a great, shapeless collection of straw, hay, paper, feathers and tufts of sheep wool, with a warm well-padded core. It contained ten naked, squirming young rats. Bodach raked out the nest with his claws and pulled it into the open. He snapped, chewed, and swallowed and he soon had the ten rats inside him. Knowing that baby rats had mothers he went back in to look for her. She was there, but digging away from him. As a digger she was not in his class and he soon had her in his jaws. Being a rat she fought him, squealing and biting as he killed her. He took the body outside and ate it.

With twenty ounces of rat inside him he was satisfied, and set out for home, travelling the road through the ride to the larch wood gate. Mathair was at the sett, reaching her height against the scratching post; Bodach scented her, then reared beside her, clawing higher. Keely arrived on the downhill trail. Mathair ran to her, and after they had grappled, and rolled together, and scented each other, they went below ground at the same entrance, leaving Bodach clawing at the post. Caileag and her twins were already abed.

Bodach syne left the post and padded to his mound, where he sat down to claw himself; the thud of his hindfoot hitting the frozen heap could be heard by the crows across the Breac. He had his head in the tunnel, ready to go below, when his ears changed his mind, and he faced about to look and listen, standing his height with his arrowhead swaying and his nostrils sifting. Boc-earb was walking towards the scratching post.

The buck prodded the post. He stabbed it hard and raked upwards, and his left antler fell off. Blood blistered from the socket and trickled, beaded, between his eye and his ear; then it congealed. If he was aware of the loss he betrayed no sign of it, for he walked away without even sniffing at the cast antler, which had blood smears on the white bone under the coronet. Bodach sat up, clawed his chest, and went to bed.

Down at Drochaid Farm Drummond was perplexed when he came with his son, armed with a pick, to barrow sand from the heap in the morning. He looked at the wreckage, recognising it for what it was, and wondered. When Nell pushed in and started to dig, he said to her:

'Leave it. There'll be nothing there noo.'

'Only somebody wi a pick could hae done that,' his son said.

'Or a badger,' Drummond reflected. 'Only a badger could hae broken into that.' Drummond was no fool in any of his three languages.

'Then it wid be a badger mair than likely that coupit the bin doon at the cottages. And there's anither thing,' he added. 'There was a wee monument on wan o the founds. The men were givin it the *Eyes Right* and bowin tae it like Japanese when I gaed by on the tractor earlier this mornin.'

Chapter Twelve

A few nights later Coll was in the larder skinning hinds when the estate factor telephoned to ask him to come along to his house after he had had his supper. There was some business he wanted to discuss. 'Take your time,' he said. 'There's no hurry. Use the Land Rover.'

After a bath and a meal Coll drove to the house, dressed in his shifting suit of plus fours, and smoking a light tobacco, thinking the factor might faint at a whiff of the bogey roll.

'Come in!' the factor greeted him. As always he was in his MacKintoch kilt. 'You'll be wondering what this sudden summons is all about?'

'The thought did cross my mind,' Coll laughed.

'Well, sit down! You'll have a dram? Good! But before I go on to business – have you seen Pharic today?'

Puzzled, Coll said: 'No! But he's coming to the house for a blether tomorrow night.'

'Well,' the factor said, 'he was in the hotel last night with Willie MacKinnon, the schoolmaster, and some University chap he had staying with him – Alec something or other and an ecologist no less – and Pharic was telling them, and I'm paraphrasing, about the badger he keeled for you, the one you let go, when who comes over and sits himself down at the next table but you know who . . . Guess?'

'I'm guessing,' Coll said. 'The *brochan* . . .?'

'The what?'

'The ither side of the Slainte.'

'Bull's eye! Well, there was seemingly a bit of an altercation. Acrimonious was the way Willie MacKinnon put it to me when he phoned me this morning. The man was positively truculent.'

'But about what?' Coll asked. 'You mean he eavesdropped on what they were talking about and butted in?'

'Bull's eye again! I'm paraphrasing, but seemingly he went on about the only good badger being a dead one – that they killed lambs and God knows what else – and that this place was a breeding ground for vermin. He said he would sort out all the eagles and peregrines and hawks and wildcats and whatever if he had his way . . .'

'Good God!' Coll said. 'And Pharic? Pharic said nothing?'

'Well, Pharic told him he was the shepherd and had never heard of a badger taking a lamb, and the University chap tried sweet reason, and Willie MacKinnon asked him to leave – but it was all a waste of time seemingly.'

'But it ended up all right?'

'Well, you could say that, depending on where you're sitting. But the man then went on to say he'd been brought up to kill all vermin.'

'So he was brought up that way,' Coll was unruffled. 'It's a point of view, but I happen not to share it.'

'Nor I, as you well know,' the factor said. 'But there was the punchline. When he said the bit about killing all vermin, Willie MacKinnon said to him: "Well, you didn't make a very good job of it, did you?" And he asked what that was supposed to mean, and Willie said to him: "Well, you're still here." '

'My God!' Coll was astonished. 'Willie? The school master! Why didn't they just ignore him?'

'Well, apparently Pharic managed to shunt him away, and get him to leave.'

'Well,' Coll said, 'now that we've had the pantomime, what about the business?'

'Of course. And what I've just told you is germane to what I have to ask. How many badgers are there on Dalnabreac?'

Coll stared at him.

'Now don't start getting the wrong idea. You'll be pleased when I tell you why I'm asking.'

'I don't know, and that's a fact. There were eight at the Breac when I last saw them. Then there's Ash Tree sett, and The Corrach, and two small ones on the far side of Ben Dearg, not counting all the odd holes they have here and there. Sixteen beasts in all, maybe . . .'

'That's your estimate?'

'That's my guess.'

'How long do you think it would take you to ascertain the exact number?'

'A gey time, and not soon. Why?'

'To find out if you've any to spare. There's a friend of the Big House has bought a place up north and he would like badgers on it. They used to be there, but they were gassed out by the old keeper. Seems a nice chap, the man who's bought the place. Lost an arm in the war. Likes badgers and would like to study them as a hobby.'

'But if there are badgers near at hand some of them will move in sooner or later.'

'Apparently there's none within fifteen miles. Could you do it?'

'I like the idea,' Coll said. 'It's nice to know there are still places where folks like to see things about. I'm sure we could give the man three, and no census needed. I'd rather see our spares flitted out than crossing the Slainte to wind up as sporrans. The best time to catch them would be winter, when they're hungry, but we'll be at the hinds till February month and that's too late.'

'Oh?'

'Because that's cubbing time and we dinna want to be catching sows that are being sooked.'

'I see. And when would be the next best time?'

'June or July month. We could check the outliers and see what's what. I wouldn't want to touch the Breac sett, for that's the main one.'

'How would you catch them?'

'You mean, how would I try? I'd use box traps. I don't like the idea of digging because that means using terriers, and terriers get cut up. I'd never send a dog of mine into a hole where I kent there was a badger. Tarf's still short of a bit neck.'

'Yes, I heard. How is she?'

'She's fine now. She might meet anither badger when we're at the foxes, but not if I ken about it first. Anyway, digging at the Breac is out of the question; the badgers have been there for a hundred years, or as Simon would say, since Pontius was a Pilate.'

'But digging them out is usual, isn't it? This box-trapping you suggest . . . isn't that a bit unorthodox?'

Coll laughed. 'Where there's a way, there's a will. My father box-trapped badgers and that wasn't the day before yesterday. I've box-trapped a fox, and a badger before. Digging was what they called a sport, and the badger was killed; now they've made it respectable by not killing the badger. But terriers still get mauled and killed. So boxing it'll have to be.'

'Good!' The factor was pleased. 'So you could start, when? We'll soon be into December. How would that suit?'

'I'll be at the hinds.'

'Yes. But supposing I stalked with Simon for a week or ten days? I haven't been out yet this season, and the exercise would do me good.' He patted his belly, which was no bigger than it ought to be. 'Would that give you enough time?'

'That would depend. I'd want to give the box a trial run, let the badgers use it and get used to it. But they're beginning to stay in more at night, and a big snow would jigger everything.'

'Right then. How long will it take to get you what you need? And remember, money's no object; the man said so. And I'm to tell you there's a case of the best malt in it for you, even for trying.'

'Oh, we won't worry about that,' Coll laughed. 'But if you get the carpenter to make me two boxes of good planking – six by fifteen inches wide by eighteen inches high, with a heavy drop door at each end – and it has to be heavy mind – I'll do the rest.'

'And help?'

'Yes, I'll need some help. Pharic would help, I'm sure. It's night work so he'll be free of the sheep. If that's all right?'

'I'm sure it will be. I'll tell him.'

'Better to ask him,' Coll said.

'Same thing. Now, you'll have another dram?'

'Thank you, yes. And one more thing. I'll be baiting the box-catchers with venison or rabbit, so I'll need a supply.'

'Take what rabbits you need from the freezer. And when you need venison, take shoulders.'

'*Slainte!*' Coll raised his glass.

'*Slainte!*' the factor replied.

Next day, at darkening, the estate pick-up arrived at the larder, where Coll and Simon were skinning hinds.

'Here's your coffins,' the driver said to Coll. 'It must be great to hae somebody by the lug in high places. Order at eight in the mornin, an delivery at five the same day.'

'We're trying tae bate the Japs,' Simon told him.

'What the hell are they for, onyway?' the driver asked.

'For my carrots. Stand them on end, fill them wi soil, an saw carrots in them. Man, I'll hae the grandest carrots, the like o whit you've never seen!'

When Pharic and Simon visited Coll later in the evening they discussed the plan for trying to box badgers.

'The trouble is,' Coll said to them, 'that the beasts stay in more at this time o year, and when they do come out they take their time about it, the nights being so long. Not like the summer, when the nights are short and they've to get on with it. And it's my opinion – if we're to catch a beast at all – it'll be as soon as it comes out. So I'd like to look the boxes a few hours after dark.'

'Fair enough,' Pharic agreed.

'So whit's the drill?' Simon asked. 'When do we tak up the coffins to catch the quick?'

'Not yet, Simon,' Coll said. 'I don't want to put them down where there are nae badgers. Tomorrow morning I'll put sticks over the setts at Ash Tree and The Corrach to find out are there badgers in them. I'll gang back late at night and if they're down I'll put them back. If they're down again in the morning, the beasts are in again. Then we'll put the coffins in place.'

'What about the Breac sett?' Pharic asked.

'I don't want to touch it if I can help it. But if the others are empty we'll think about it. Mind you, I'd want to know how many are in it first. There were eight the last time I was at it.'

Pharic sipped his dram. 'So we put the boxes down and the beasts walk in?'

'That's the idea,' Coll agreed.

'Wi baits in them?' Simon asked.

'That's right. We'll let the beasts go in and out for a night or two first, then we'll set the drop door.'

'And doon goes the guillotine,' Pharic laughed.

'And draps on the badger's neck,' Simon added.

'No,' said Coll. 'The bait'll be at the ither end, so the beast'll have to go richt ben to reach it. That's why the boxes are six feet long.'

'And you'll need me – when?' Pharic asked.

'When we take up the boxes,' Coll told him. 'And after that if we catch a badger. But one beast's no good to us. We've got to catch a pair or three. We'll take Blossom off the hinds for a day to get the boxes up, and give Simon another pony. Blossom's reliable.'

'She'll gang by hersel,' Simon said, 'if you just lay oot a trail o sugar lumps from here to the setts.'

'Well,' observed Pharic, 'she's carried a wheen dead beasts off the hill, but this'll be the first time she's delivered coffins.'

In the morning Coll helped Simon and the ponyman saddle the ponies Donald, Hector, Bluebell and Blossom. Drummond's son arrived on a tractor; he had come to help with the ponies for the day. The two set off on their long trek to the hill, each leading two ponies in tandem. When the factor arrived Coll handed him rifle and cartridges, then joined him with Simon in the Land Rover. They drove to the far end of the new road through the ride at Drochaid and left it there.

'Well, I'll leave you chaps here,' Coll said. 'I'm for through the wood.' He looked at his watch. 'I should catch up with you in two, two and a half hours or so.'

'No hurry,' Simon said, waving to him.

At Ash Tree Coll looked over the holes and knew at once that badgers had been working at it, but he wanted to be sure they were there. He broke off finger-thick pine twigs, shaved them to clean sticks with his gralloching knife, and wedged them upright, four inches apart, like prison bars over the holes. Any badger emerging would have to knock them down or aside.

Next he went to The Corrach sett, which also had what he called a used look about it, and put sticks over the holes there too. Siskins were flitting and pecking in the birches, and he could hear goldcrests in the pines. Although the Breac was iced over, and the wood rimed grey and silver, the frost had pulled in its claws, as he could tell by the tips of his fingers and ears. A heron rose as he was crossing the Breac footbridge, and he spoke to it: 'It's the pneumatic drill you'll need to get into that today, my lad.'

He crossed the grassland to the Piper's Cairn, and from there spied along the Slainte and up to Ben Dearg. There was no sign of Simon or the factor, but he could see the ponies, still being led in tandem, on the near side of the scree, making up and across. The light wind was coming at him, so he knew it was safe to go on; the men would be on the other side of the ridge, stalking away from him.

On the ridge he bellied down and spied ahead. Now he could see the stalkers, and two parcels of hinds far below them – upwind and out of sight. Presently he saw a thin column of

144

smoke, like an Indian signal, and he knew that was Simon's sign to the ponyman to come on. Coll rose, slung the glass, and set out at a brisk pace towards the ponies. He met them a few hundred yards from the stalkers, who had two hinds down and gralloched, ready to be loaded on the ponies.

'We had wan apiece from the first parcel,' Simon greeted Coll. 'Good beasts too, and fat. The Deutschers'll be made up wi them.'

'Would you like me to take over now?' Coll asked the factor.

'No,' he said. 'I'm fine. I'll stick with it.'

'Fine,' Coll said. 'If we put this two on Blossom, I'll take her home and get them skinned and hung. That'll leave you chaps a bit freer,' he said to young Drummond and the ponyman.

Coll left with Blossom while Simon began the stalk into the next group of hinds. Carrying two hinds was no problem for the strong, willing mare, but Coll took her home at an easy pace. He had thought for all the ponies, but he was byornar fond of Blossom, and thought it must have been a horse like her that Orwell had in mind when he created Boxer in *Animal Farm*. Simon said she was a four-legged tractor, wi mair between her ears than ony fowr heids at Westminster. At the larder Coll unslung the hinds, and unsaddled her. Then he put her in a lean-to shed, wiped her down with some clean straw, hayed and watered her, and gave her some bruised oats. 'D'you think that'll haud ye till ye get your richt supper?' he said to her. She nickered to him, nosing the oats.

Three hours after dark Coll was at the Ash Tree sett, where he found his sticks thrust aside; so the badgers were out, or had been out and in again. He put the sticks back in place. At The Corrach the sticks were down at one hole, and he replaced them too. After daylight he visited both setts, and found the sticks pushed aside again. So he reckoned the badgers were at home.

On the Saturday, after Pharic had been to the hill, and Simon was free, they put the deer saddle on Blossom and fixed the boxes in place, one firmly secured along each flank. She looked round at them, as though wondering what kind of deer she was being loaded with; but she stood as placidly as ever, and moved off quietly when asked – led by Coll, with Pharic and Simon flanking her to keep an eye on the boxes. They unloaded one box at Ash Tree, and the other at The Corrach. In one box were two spades, some stakes, and a stob mell. Pharic left the others to put the boxes in place and took Blossom home.

Coll and Simon levelled off a base for the boxes at Ash Tree and The Corrach, and set them in position. They drove two stakes into the ground, on both sides of each, so that they could not be moved or rolled over by the badgers. Coll rubbed deer fat on the floor inside the entrances, then pushed the venison baits to the closed ends with his stick. There no badger could reach them from the entrances; the beast would have to walk right in.

'That's that, then,' Coll said to Simon. 'We'll see what's what in the morning.'

But he did not wait for morning. After snatching a hasty bite at home he returned to Ash Tree – warmly clad, with corduroy shorts under his plus-fours and the flaps of his two-snooter down over his ears – and climbed to a thick branch twelve feet from the ground, on which he sat down to wait. The sun was near setting and a misshapen moon rising in a clear sky. He was looking down at the open end of the box, and watching the entrances to the sett for the first flicker of white in profile.

Two hours later he saw it, but not at one of the holes. It was coming up the trail from the fork, bob-bob-bobbing – the arrow-head of Bodach, homing fast on Ash Tree for a visit. Instead of going below ground he stopped opposite the entrance to the box, half turned towards it, lowered his head and sniffed. He walked over to it and pushed his arrowhead in to the shoulders. Coll tensed on his seat. He wanted to cough, but smothered it by swallowing hard. Bodach walked into the box, and syne backed out again, with a piece of venison in his mouth. He carried it into cover and lay down to eat it.

By cricks, Coll thought to himself, *if I'd had the trap set I could have caught this one tonight.*

While he was thinking this thought, and Bodach chewing out of sight, a white face appeared at the nearest hole. The beast came out and scratched itself, and Coll could see its snort

146

breaths condensing on the air. Suddenly it stopped scratching and sniffed towards the box. While it was sniffing, a second badger came out of the same hole and joined it. They were Mathair's rising ten-months-old cubs. They walked to the box together. One pushed in and the other followed, and Coll could hear the scratching and thudding of them, and their low growls and brumblings as they clawed at the baits. Syne they backed out, both with a mouthful, and porpoised into cover.

Coll thought again to himself: *I could have had a pair at one go if I'd had the drop door in place and a cord in my hand*. It was an idea, and he stored it, although he was sure he would never get the same chance again.

The three badgers appeared again. One at a time they explored the box, and one at a time they withdrew. They played, and chased each other, round the base of Coll's tree, making as much noise as stirks, then Bodach padded on the down trail to the fork and the cubs went back to bed. Coll, feeling the cold in fingers and toes, sipped a little whisky from his flask, and decided to wait on, in case the badgers came out again. He did not want to be caught when he was climbing down from the tree.

Half an hour later, with no badger showing, he was ready to leave, when a big fox appeared from the cover behind the closed end of the box and approached it. He was a big dog fox, long-legged, in plush coat with thick, white-tipped brush, and he could smell venison above the ground reek of badger: but he had no warning of the man in the tree. He walked round the box, checking it over with his nose, then bellied down at the open end and sniffed into the tunnel. The venison smell was there, and he inched in up to his neck. *This won't do*, said Coll to himself under his breath. He called out: 'Get the hell out of it!' – and the fox was up and away in one graceful movement, light-footed, hardly seeming to touch the ground as he vanished into the moonlit wood.

Coll climbed down, stamped his feet and flapped his arms, and followed the badger trail to the fork, where he turned right for The Corrach. Near the sett he stopped, and watched for some minutes, but he could see no badgers on foot. He walked to the box, knelt down at the entrance and shone his pencil torch inside. The baits had all been taken. He smiled to himself and started out on the long walk home.

'I think we can speed things up a bit,' he told Simon later in the evening. 'I had three badgers exploring the box at Ash Tree and the baits were away at The Corrach. I'll phone Pharic and we'll try for real tomorrow.'

'On the sabbath?'

'You ken what they say: the better the day the better the deed. It's in a good cause.'

On the phone Pharic asked: 'When will you be leaving?'

'I thought if we left about eight, that would still leave you time to get round the sheep. Then we gang up again before badger light.'

'All right,' Pharic agreed. 'Eight o'clock it is, then.'

In the morning they went first to Ash Tree. Simon tied two chunks of venison shoulder with string, and knotted the loose ends together. He raised the drop door at the far end, laid the baits in place, then slammed it down, with the knot on the outside.

'It'll tak them a while to loosen that lot,' he said. 'Now what?'

'Give me the bobbin of twine,' Coll said. Simon handed it to him. 'Now I'm going up in the tree and try to get the end of this through that fork up there. When I do, you can tie it to the top of the door. I want to work this one by hand.'

He climbed into the tree, tied his gralloching knife to the end of the string and aimed it at the fork. It missed. He wound it in again and tried a second time. It missed. At the third throw it landed beside the entrance to the box.

'Now,' said Coll. 'Tie it to the door, and raise the door to leave two inches in the slots. I'll put a strain on here and half-hitch the end to this branch.'

Simon fixed the string and raised the drop door. Coll released the half-hitch and the door dropped like a guillotine. They tried it a second time and the door dropped again. Coll fixed the end of the string to the branch and climbed down.

'That seems all right now,' he said. 'Now for The Corrach.'

At The Corrach they baited the trap and set it up as a self-catcher. If a badger snatched the tied bait it would release the slack and the door would drop. They tried it twice from the far end and it worked. So they set it up again and left it.

Coll and Pharic were back at The Corrach when the red sun was low in the west. Pharic climbed into his tree. Coll hurried back to Ash Tree and was on his seat before the sun went down. Two hoodies, roosting uphill from him, knew he was there and were saying so. Sealgair the tawny owl was calling down near the Breac, where he was hunting water voles.

A bright moon, slimmer than on the night before, was above the trees before the first white face appeared. Coll could feel the beating of his heart, and reached for the half-hitch holding the string. The badger came out, scratched, walked to the box, and went inside, and Coll could hear it clawing at the bait. A second badger came out, walked round the box, and started scratching at the closed end. *That's real like the thing*, Coll thought to himself. Should he drop the door and make sure of one, or wait for two and perhaps lose both? He decided to wait. The second badger left the end of the box, sniffed round to the entrance, and walked in. Coll released the string almost before its scut disappeared. The door dropped. He had two badgers in the box.

Coll came down from his seat in a hurry, skinning his right shin. The badgers were thumping and clawing in the box. He slapped a palm on the flat top and the commotion ceased. Then he thought of Pharic. They had fixed no time to meet up again. Had Pharic had any luck? Coll decided to risk going to The Corrach to find out. Two hundred yards from the sett he sat down, intending to give Pharic another half hour. He lit his pipe, and within a minute Pharic appeared.

'I was sitting here for a bit to give you more time,' said Coll.

'I was doing the same back there. Then I saw your match. How'd you get on?'

'I've got two badgers!'

'Good for you. I've got one.' Pharic sounded pleased. 'And guess what?'

'What?'

'It's the one I keeled!'

'Hell, no!' Coll exclaimed. 'We don't want to part with that one.'

'What do we do then?'

'If we turn her loose now we'll maybe just catch her again. We'll take her home and hold her, and try for another one. That's if you don't mind going through all this again.'

'That's fine with me,' Pharic said. 'Will this lot be all right till morning?'

'I think so, yes. But we'll leave with Blossom about six. It'll mean coming up in the dark but the light'll be coming at us.'

They took Blossom to The Corrach and Ash Tree in the morning and brought in the three badgers, installing them in the dog kennel where Keely had been before. Pharic shook out a bale and a half of straw and they burrowed into it. Coll put in three rabbits and a heavy trough with water and locked the door.

'Don't be in a hurry back from the hill,' he told Pharic. 'I'll manage a box back up there myself.'

At mid-day he drove Blossom in the horse box to the Drochaid ride, and strapped a box on to her there. At The Corrach he set it down, baited, as before, and that night it caught a badger: the boar that Bodach had driven from the Breac. The next night he released Kelly at the larch wood badger gate.

Chapter Thirteen

On the Sunday Pharic keeled the three badgers before they were boxed for transport – the boar on the rump and Mathair's cubs, which were both sows, on the back of the neck. There and then Simon christened them The Inkspots. Neither sow showed the slightest sign of aggression when Coll pushed them into one of the catchers and dropped the door. The boar snapped once when he was being put in a reinforced tea chest. Although Coll was pleased that the beasts were going to a safe place for restocking, he had a vague feeling of regret about transplanting them so far away. With the Land Rover loaded, he said to Simon:

'Right, Simon, let's get yokit. We've sixty miles to go.'

They were met by the laird himself – a tall lean man, with grizzled hair and steady eyes that could look you in the face. Coll noticed the artificial hand protruding from the right sleeve of his Lovat jacket. He greeted them warmly.

'I'm Fitzroy Stewart,' he said. He looked at Coll: 'And you're . . .?'

'MacDonald,' Coll replied. 'Coll MacDonald.'

'So this must be Simon Fraser?' He looked at Simon, then held out his left hand to both. 'You'll excuse the boy scout handshake,' he laughed, 'but I've mislaid the other one somewhere. I'm glad to see you, Coll; I've heard a lot about you.'

'Maistly guid, I trummle,' Coll slid as smoothly into Scots as an otter into a pool.

'Indeed yes,' said Stewart. 'Well, we're in your hands with this one. We can get the Land Rover to within a hundred yards of the sett. But first – a dram and a spot of lunch?'

Over lunch Coll asked: 'How long since this sett had badgers in it?'

'Three years, I'm told. The keeper gassed them out.'

'What's the score now?'

'There's no keeper now,' said Stewart. 'I'm not concerned with sport. I've a breeding herd of Angus cattle. We get some hinds on the ground and take out two or three for the freezer. Other than that I'm not bothered.'

Coll rose. Simon said: 'Weel, whit aboot gettin the mortgages made oot and we'll get thur chaps into their hooses?'

'Have you a few rabbits, or the like?' Coll asked Stewart. 'And a bale of good straw? The beasts'll need a bed.'

'No problem,' Stewart said.

The old sett was on a slope with a burn at the bottom, in seventeen acres of mixed woodland. There were five entrances, with mounds mossed over and unmarked. Coll scraped at one with a foot, uncovering a few stained bones and rotting feathers.

'I see the fox has been here too,' he said. 'Well, Simon, let's get the boxes up.'

They tipped all three badgers into one hole, and a rabbit into three. Simon cut loose the bale of straw and laid pads along the frontage. 'That should haud them,' he said. 'Looks a grand place tae me. If they're wyce they'll stay.'

'You'll have noticed,' Coll said to Stewart, 'that we've keeled them blue, so you'll ken them if you see them. The ones keeled on the neck are the sows.'

'I hope to see a lot of them in the evenings,' Stewart said.

'Well, I think I'd leave them for a bit to settle . . .'

152

'Of course!' Stewart agreed.

'But you'll ken they're there still if they've got the straw in tomorrow. You could tak a look some time during the day.'

'Yes, I'll do that. And I'm very grateful to you chaps for all your trouble.'

'It's been oor pleasure,' Coll told him. 'And by the bye: the keel marks should last into next summer until they moult out.'

'A grand-like kind of chap, whit!' Simon said to Coll on the drive home. 'And nae miserable, either!' He reached round and patted the two cardboard cartons in the back of the Land Rover.

'A man of his word, whatever,' Coll agreed. 'And grand pleased wi a thing.'

'Twentyfowr bottles of straight malt.'

'That's right. Eight for Pharic, eight for you, and eight for me.'

A week later the factor telephoned Coll. 'I've just had the major on the phone,' he said.

'The major?'

'Yes. Fitzroy Stewart.'

'Oh! He didn't say.'

'That's like him,' the factor said. 'Well, I'm to let you know that the badgers have settled. He saw them last night. It seems they came out for a spell, and pottered about, then went back into the den.'

'I'm very glad to hear that,' said Coll.

'I thought you would be.'

Chapter Fourteen

A feeding storm of rain, hail and sleet, with frost and morning cramassie, hanselled the time of long sleeping for the Breac badgers; when lying abed, burning their fat slowly, was a surer way of staying alive and fit than running it off on fruitless forays during nights of iron-clad ground or blanket snow. For five nights they stayed below, sleeping deeply or fitfully, and not a white face showing, while the wind raked the hill, howling like a wolf pack in the high corries and wailing its coronach in The Corrach pines. On the sixth morning, when the sky cleared, the oakwood was in cranreuch and the Breac running silent under glass ice feathered and veined with white. Before nightfall, in brief tantrum, the wind powdered the cranreuch with the first tracking snow.

Bodach peered out at the howdumdeid on a white, silent world freezing under a starlit sky in which a pale moon gleamed. The shadow of Sealgair the tawny owl wavered over the mound in front of his face and he pulled back, startled; but presently his face appeared again, and a few minutes later he padded to the scratching post where he reared to claw his height. Syne Mathair, Keely and Caileag surfaced, and after they had clawed themselves and the post the four reared, grappled and climbed over each other in friendly bourach. When they separated Bodach turned away downhill, breathing out jets of vapour. The sows, after staining the snow with their urine, went back to bed.

Fox, roe, stoat and rabbit had already printed the snow with their tracks, which were hardening like plaster casts in the eggshell frost crust: round the oaks wound the necklaces left by woodmice feet. On the way to the Breac Bodach left hand-footed tracks where he walked, and multiple grooves cut by his claws where he skidded on the icy, downhill trail. The shadows of the burnside alders lay hard and dark aslant the snow; in one of them fieldfares were roosting, all facing uphill. Elderberry clusters, frosted and dropping from bare branches, looked like roosting bats. Bodach walked on to the ice, sat down, and sniffed in a half circle. He could smell water vole.

The vole was sitting on a raft of frozen rushes under the bank, his fur shark-toothed by the shadows of grass blades above him. He was feeding one-handed – nibbling on a grass blade held in one forefoot and stroking his flank fur with the other. Bitten stems were lying on the raft beside him. Bodach put a foot forward. The vole dropped the grass blade he was nibbling and craned forward, listening. Bodach leaped towards him, at a speed surprising for his bulk; but the vole was no longer there. He was away into his burrow, on the doorstep of which he had been feeding.

Bodach started to claw at the hole, where the musty smell was tantalisingly fresh; but the ground here was harder than the sand-heap at Drochaid Farm, and he quickly gave up. He mounted the bank and dug there, but after scraping out a trench three feet long and four inches deep he gave that up too, and returned to the ice. He yawned and scratched then walked upstream, leaving his tracks on the feathering. At the first pool he found a heron under an overhanging alder; it was frozen in standing, emaciated and dying, slumped forward with its head on the ice, its beak open and its eyes closed to slits. Lean with famine, hungered and unalert, it had stood under the alder while the ice formed round its legs. Bodach killed it quickly with a neck bite and snapped its legs like sticks, leaving its feet locked in the ice. There was little on the heron except skin and bone, but he ate what was eatable and returned to the sett. He had been less than an hour above ground.

In murky morning calm came more snow like a leaf-fall, draping the pines in white ostrich plumes and limning the oaks to dark fretted skeletons. When it ceased the only black patches on the mantled ground were the entrances to the badger sett. By moonrise the ostrich plumes on the pines were frozen and every oak twig furred in ermine. Bodach came out in snow up to his elbows and plodded to his scratching post, drawing out a deep furrow behind him; Mathair appeared and followed it to join him. Together they rolled in the snow and bit it. When Bodach stood up he had a white fluff on his nose, which he scraped off with a paw. Then the pair followed the furrow back to their tunnel and went to bed. Neither Keely nor Caileag had stirred from their sleeping nests.

That first snowfall made the hind stalking difficult but did not stop it, and Coll and Simon went to the hill with ear flaps of two snooters down and woollen hoggers over their boots and legs. They came in at dusk with their tweed fronts stiff with wind-blasted snow, and frosted clots like ectoparasites clinging to their hoggers. The belly and leg hairs of the ponies Bluebell and Blossom were icicled, and Simon rubbed them off with his hands, saying: 'Stand still dames while I tak aff your sleigh bells!'

Coll and Simon were expecting a bigger snow and a halt to the stalking. Instead, a thawing westerly brought days and nights of rain, and the snow shrank on ridges and south-facing slopes. Mallards splashed and guttered in shallow pools on the Breac ice; tits and siskins flitted again in the oakwood. After one rain storm the clouds opened a blue clearing of sky, and a watergaw straddled Ben Dearg, in unbroken arc, framing an eagle and two ravens soaring. White hares hopped from the concealing snow ground to forage betrayed on dark areas cleared by rain and thaw.

The badgers came out on the soft nights of mud glidder between storms of rain, staining with their hand-feet the snow beside their trails, near which they left many scrapes, ringed with dark soil, where they had dug for bluebell bulbs, roots and earthworms. On the uphill trail, below the eagle's rock, Mathair found a rabbit, killed and partly eaten by Fraioch the stoat, which she dragged into cover and devoured down to the last nail and wisp of fur. Across the Breac, near the stepping stones, Bodach nosed out a dead redwing in a bramble patch. He ripped feathers from it, and ate the body, leaving only the wings.

Towards the year's end the real winter arrived on a wind like liquid glass that froze the glen. Then the snow came – blizzard mounting on blizzard till only the crag faces showed black on the hill. Between blizzards a hurricane wind drifted the snow, sculpting it into razor-backed dunes, escarpments and cornices, and burying the badger sett. Red deer trekked from the hill, dark shapes moving in clouds of breath and hoof-stirred snow. With them came the hares of the mountain, singly and in twos and threes – leaping, white-furred ghostly shapes on snow-shoe feet. Foxes, gaunt and hungry, followed the hares. Even the white ptarmigan came down to join the red grouse in the heather along the Slainte.

The red stags milled in The Corrach, where they trod out lanes to browse and forage; a parcel of hinds gathered in the oakwood between the badger sett and the eagle's crag. Boc-earb harboured in The Corrach, under the ample spread of a big spruce, surrounded by scatterings of his own droppings. Capercaillies and black grouse burrowed into the snow. In the heather the red grouse trampled it as it fell, and when the wind died and the sky cleared they were crouched in half-igloos of heather, roofed over with snow. Fraioch the stoat, now in ermine, padded over the drifts, or hunted under them for vole or woodmouse. On the drifts he was invisible when still; moving, he was betrayed by his black tail-tip, stalking him like a camp follower.

During the long nights of wind and snow no badger left the

sett, and only Bodach stirred to unblock the entrance to his tunnel. He scraped the loose snow on to the mound, discolouring it with the soil on his pads. One day Coll visited the sett, high-stepping on home made snow-shoes, and was surprised to see a single dark hole on the white brae face, because he thought it meant that the badgers had been out; but when he found no tracks on the yowdendrift he came to the conclusion that they had opened it to admit air. Uphill and down were deer and fox slots, the prints of hare and rabbit and woodmice chains, but not a single foot-sign of a badger.

Night frosts silvered the oakwood and crusted the snow; new falls, wind blown and sharp as sand, blotted out the tracks, and everywhere there was ice. It glassed and ribbed the rocks and sealed the oak buds. Icicles like walrus tusks appeared on the eagle's rock where water had dripped. Five minutes before year's end Bodach climbed out on to the drift covering his mound and scratched himself, sending snowballs like hazel nuts rolling downhill. After sitting up to sniff and listen he ploughed his way to the uphill trail, and was above his tunnel entrance when he heard the twin pops of a shotgun coming faintly from Drochaid. Drummond, in traditional style, was saluting the new year with his twelvebore.

Bodach paused and listened, not alarmed, then started uphill, sinking to wrist and ankle in the snow crust. He knew where he was going. At the top of the slope, near the eagle's crag, was a thicket of dogrose and bramble. Long tendrils of dogrose, still carrying a richness of rimed, hard hips, were trailing on the snow, and Bodach had before him an easy harvest for which he had neither to reach up nor dig. He began to snip off doghips, one at a time, munching and swallowing, discarding nothing. Mathair, Keely and Caileag arrived, and syne four badgers were bellied down round the thicket, gathering hips at ground level. It was not often that they could gorge on doghips, which were usually out of their reach, and when within reach still had their daunting defence of thorns like the teeth of foxes.

Boc-earb, in early velvet, was also feeding on doghips, ignoring the badgers and being ignored by them: he was well

158

rumped, fat-ribbed and not haughty. Five red deer hinds and three calves were cudding browse and grass under the eagle's rock, with ears up and breath vapouring. The white hares had moved uphill, clear of the trees. Sealgair the tawny owl was *wee-wicking* in a stag-headed oak, listening, and watching for vole or mouse movement on the snow: his craw was empty and his cat calls a plaint.

Bodach was the first to leave the dogrose thicket, and took the downhill trail, which was now a trampled, shallow furrow; near the sett it was stained with earth brought out by the badgers on their feet. Instead of going to ground he furrowed his way down to the Breac, where he licked ice and nibbled at hazel catkins. When he returned to the sett the three sows were there, and Mathair was clawing snow from another entrance. The one from which all four had emerged was churned and stained. Bodach went in at his own entrance, the sows into the one opened by Mathair.

Another heavy snowfall brought the hares into the oakwood again, and the black grouse to the alders. On a clear starlit night, with the sky like mole's fur, Bodach furrowed his way through soft snow to the Breac. Fraioch the stoat was stalking over the drifts, and in a snow burrow caught a late-born leveret, which she killed by a bite on the neck. She dragged the body into the open, and ate what she could of it – which was nearly a third of her own weight – then hefted the remainder back into the burrow and scraped snow over it. Bodach, returning uphill on the furrowed trail, smelled both stoat and leveret and uncovered her cache. Being empty-bellied he ate what was left of the leveret, leaving only bloodstains and wool fluffs for Fraioch to find when she returned to her kill.

More snow fell and drifted and for eight days the badgers remained below ground, but once again Bodach bored through to the open to unblock the entrance to his tunnel. When the thaw came it came suddenly, with a west wind followed by drizzling rain. The walrus tusks on the eagle's crag crashed: the ice on the Breac thinned and mallards guttered and spluttered in the shallow, surface pools. Water song was heard again on the hill and syne the Breac, snow-fed, was reaming. Coll and Simon returned to the stalking – in sunshine, wind, rain and sudden blasts of sleet. It was four weeks to the season's end and they still had twenty hinds to kill.

One morning, stalking round Ben Dearg, they found badger tracks above the heather line, half a mile from the cliff where Pharic's lamb had fallen to its death. At two thousand feet the tracks turned back, diagonally towards the Piper's Cairn. Coll would have liked to follow them down, but Blossom was loaded and he had to go the opposite way. He spied down to the Piper's Cairn then round to the cliff.

'There must be a beast dead below the wee cliff,' he said to Simon. 'There's ravens and crows below it and an eagle on top.'

'What the hell is a badger daein awa oot here in weather like this?' Simon said. 'Unless it's maybe a boar efter a mate.'

'Could be a sow on the same ploy,' Coll replied. 'But why should it turn back here? I wouldn't wonder, Simon, if these tracks lead to the wee cliff. I wonder . . .?'

'Look,' Simon said, 'I'll carry on hame wi the ponyman and Blossom, and you go doon and see. If you take The Corrach road home, you'll be at the larder before us onyway.'

Coll started down and across towards the wee cliff, and presently the badger tracks curved to join his line. They led to the cliff. The eagle, ravens and crows flew away when they saw the man approaching. At the bottom of the cliff lay a hind and her calf, half buried in snow, each with the exposed eye missing. They had been trapped by an avalanche. Coll followed the badger tracks, first to the hollow where Pharic had buried the lamb, then to the bridge over the Breac, and through The Corrach to the stepping stones where Bodach had crossed.

Highland badgers often go high at the tail end of winter and in early spring, when they can be tracked for many miles in the snow; but only Bodach knew why he had travelled to two thousand feet on Ben Dearg in the middle of January while deer, hares and even ptarmigan were still on lower slopes. On

160

the way up he had missed the dead hind and calf; his nose told him about them when he was homing, and he had detoured to eat venison. Two hours after being tracked home by Coll be was on his way back to the cliff. Whether by desire for his company, or by some kind of communication, Mathair followed some distance behind him, and later in the night they were joined at the cliff by Caileag and Keely.

Just about everything that eats flesh will eat venison, right down to woodmice and shrews. Foxes like it; wildcats like it; eagles, buzzards, ravens and crows like it, and any one of them can be readily trapped at a venison bait. Badgers like it, but probably taste it less often than the others. Being night hunters they have to find it for themselves, unlike the hill cats and foxes which, prowling by day in the stalking season, are often guided to it by the carrion birds.

When Bodach arrived a fox was eating from the calf. She snarled at him and tried to pull it away, but could not move it. Bodach started on the hind, biting at the back of the haunch, near the tail, where the ravens and crows had done their beak surgery on it during the day. The eagle had torn flesh there too, working along the spine towards the hip. Mathair arrived, drove the fox from the calf and settled down to eat. When Caileag and Keely appeared they joined Bodach at the hind. The vixen sat back, with her tongue out, content to wait until they left. She knew there was enough to go round many times.

The venison was a godsend to the sows. They needed it more than Bodach, for their pregnancies were developing rapidly from the blastocysts implanted in their wombs during the last week of the old year. They gorged, and left, carrying nothing away. Bodach did not follow them. He scraped in the place where Pharic had buried the lamb, clawing out stones and the witherings and roots of wild thyme. When he had made enough room for himself he moved in and faced out, pulling stones and wild thyme remains towards him, and behind this screening frontage he slept fitfully, not warm but not cold, until he was awakened by ravens croaking in the morning twilight.

With all the confidence of total ownership Pruk and Borb

pitched beside the carcasses and waggle-swaggered round them, nodding their heads and chuckling as though considering where to begin work. Syne they picked their places, Pruk at the navel of the hind and Borb on the rump – stabbing, probing, excising and swallowing. Having nothing else to do they took their time; and having so much meat before them they became choosy, tossing aside unwanted morsels. Every now and again they stopped to look around them with far-seeing ramgumptious eyes. If they were thinking, which is unlikely, they would be thinking they had it all to themselves; if they were not thinking, which is more likely, they would be assuming it. But they were wrong. The venison magnet was drawing in others.

A big mountain fox, with white ruff, white-tipped brush, and red legs with only anklets of black, came homing in, guided unerringly by his nose. He had nothing in his belly but much in his head, and when he mounted a boulder to survey the scene he knew after two looks and three sniffs exactly what he was going to do; and he did it. He trotted unhesitatingly up to the carcass, showed his teeth to the ravens, and they lifted aside, croaking, with their head and neck feathers raised. They did not like the intrusion, and displayed their dislike by the way they hackled up and tossed twigs and stones around. But they had something in their bellies, and were prepared to put up with it – for the moment.

The fox bit into the hind near the tail, where there was now plenty of clearway, but although he buried his muzzle in it he kept an eye on the ravens. Nothing with any sense ignores ravens, and this fox had sense in abundance. He was five years old and ignored nothing; which is why he was five. Pruk and Borb side-stepped round him and started to stab at the calf. The fox raised his head to see what they were doing then went back to his eating.

Iolair the eagle flew over at first light and the ravens tilted their heads to look up at him. The fox did not look up; he carried on biting and burrowing. But he was still watching the ravens, while making a great show of ignoring them. So when they began to edge round to get behind him he pulled out, and moved to the hind's belly, where Pruk had already holed it. Now he was squatted at right angles to the deer – biting, worrying, pulling, and shaking his head; but still watching the ravens. It was then that Bodach lumbered from his hiding place, blinking, yawning and stretching himself.

The ravens flapped aside to strut, long-necking and making rattling noises in their throats, not afraid of the badger, but perhaps a little alarmed at having been caught off guard. The fox raised his head, pricked his ears, and back-tracked a few paces to see what he would do. Bodach padded over to the hind carcass and began to eat from the haunch; the fox moved forward again on to the calf. That left the ravens as spectators. They had seen a badger before, but always at dusk, when they were at roost, so Bodach was outside their experience. A fox they knew how to deal with; of the badger they were not so sure.

The sun came up like a monstrous flower, blinding with its glare. Its light crept along the base of the cliff, spotlighting deer, ravens, badger and fox. Bodach blinked, and turned his back to it. The dark, shadowy ravens now glowed purple, with the light glancing on their ebony beaks; the shadowy fox became red, with grey on his flanks, and a star in his amber eyes. Bodach faced the glare, blinked, turned away and ran to his hole under the rock, which was in shadow. He faced about, gathered his screen, and watched.

The fox returned to the hind, and the ravens moved in closer. Almost inevitably he took his mind off them for a moment and was caught off guard. Pruk lifted into the air and swooped at his rump. The strike brought his head up, but even as he turned, chopping and flashing his teeth, Borb was in and tweaked his tail, and that put him in a rage. He rushed at one then the other, which was a waste of his time. They began to play with him. They touched down in front of his face and taunted him; they lifted away and swooped at him; they joined in converging attack on his rump. He ducked and dodged and bellied down, making threatening noises with his teeth; but they were not impressed. In the end he sneaked away a few paces and lay down against a boulder. From there he snarled at them with his eyes slitted, but that made as little impression on them as his teeth clicking. They swaggered to the carcass of the hind and dabbed at it, not eating because they were no longer hungry.

They were now pouching food, and once their beaks and pouches were full they had to fly somewhere to cache it. While they were gone Fior-eun the eagle swooshed down and thudded on to the hind carcass. Bodach, dozing after watching the ravens and the fox, was brought wide awake again. Fior-eun hopped to the ground, turned about flat-footed and ponderously, and began to tear at the hind's belly with her beak. She was the mighty one, in possession; the lordly queen of the air that none dare question. And lordly and queenly she was until the ravens came back.

They came in on her at low level, one behind the other, not striking her but barely missing her. They swept up, and round, and swooped again, this time letting their undercarriages down and touching her with their talons. Fior-eun turned about awkwardly, spreading her wings, facing for a downhill take-off. But there was no downhill. The ground below the cliff was a depression and she had to run – hop, skip and jump – with her wings open, the queen dethroned, until she reached a hummock from which she could launch away. The ravens followed her as she soared, and dived when she dived. They overflew her; they underflew her; they outflew her. Up and up they went, to the height of Ben Dearg; then down they came, diving and spiralling, back to the carcass, to pouch more food and carry it away.

All day carrion birds came to the carcasses, ate and left. At one time there were five ravens on the hind and three hoodie crows on the calf. At mid-afternoon, when the ground from the cliff to the Slainte was in shadow, Iolair and Fior-eun pitched on the hind, and presently a bitch fox approached stealthily to the calf and bellied down beside it. The eagles watched her, and she watched them. She was wary of them, even afraid. No sane fox would think of facing an eagle, even a grounded one, and when Fior-eun took a step towards her – with wings half open and neck feathers raised: a thing of power with rending beak and feet like grappling hooks – she backed away from the calf. Then Fior-eun lost interest, and began to tear at the hind. Warily, the fox bellied back to the calf.

When the eagles ground-flapped to a boulder for a launching take-off Bodach came out: the ground between him and the cliff was now in heavy shadow. He walked to the hind, stood by the rump, and ripped down a large patch of skin, tugging with all his strength and baring a bigger area of flesh. He could see and smell the vixen, but paid no heed to her; they were not in competition. Then he winded something else and lifted his head. The smell was cat, and it was coming to him from the boulder where the dog fox had taken refuge from the ravens.

He was a big cat, all Highland, with moon eyes, ears at ease, and teeth locked away: not the flat-eared grimacing stereotype beloved of artists and photographers. He knew the venison was there, and was hungry for it; but he could see the fox and the badger, and that put him off. So he was content to wait on, cat patient, knowing that the fox and badger would go away and the venison would not.

The vixen left first, carrying a mouthful of venison, and the cat prudently climbed down from the boulder and crawled under it. He feared no fox, but he trusted none either. With her stomach and mouth full of meat the vixen had time for the nonsense that sometimes enters the heads of foxes. At five she should have known better. She padded to the boulder, laid down her mouthful, crouched beside the hole and looked in; and there they were, like cat and dog in the oldest game in the world. The cat slitted his eyes, flattened his ears, bared his teeth, and wailed his war-song. The vixen nosed closer, and again she should have known better. The cat reached out an armed forepaw, cuffed at her, and exploded in her face. That put the nonsense out of her head. She picked up her mouthful and trotted away.

Syne Bodach withdrew to his shelter to wait for dusk. The big cat came out of hiding and panthered to the calf. She was still bristling, and glared back at the boulder before settling to eat. At darkening Bodach left his shelter and shambled away on The

165

Corrach trail; he had had enough of lying out in such an unbieldy bed. All the wrangling and cangling he had heard, sensed or seen were meaningless to him; he was the great neutral, concerned with food and nobody else's affairs.

At The Corrach footbridge he met Mathair on her way to the cliff; they touched noses in greeting and set scent on the snow and each other. Near Ash Tree he met Caileag and Keely, following Mathair's trail, and he greeted them too. Then he trotted home to bed – a badger with his normal timetable reversed.

Chapter Fifteen

The thaw cleared the Breac, except for patches of white in hollows and in the shade of rocks. Before the end of the stalking season Bodach made one more foray over the high snow of Ben Dearg, and Coll and Simon saw his outgoing and return tracks when they were crossing above the wee cliff to meet the ponyman beside a hind they had killed and gralloched earlier. The gralloch had slid downhill on the packed snow, leaving a trail of blood smears and clots, and Pruk the raven flew to it not long after the men and the pony had gone. His mate Borb was at the nest, not hunting because she was ready to lay her first egg.

She was standing guard over four when Mathair gave birth to twins in the Breac sett – blind, mewing things like short-coupled piglets, big-headed, less than six inches long, with thin greyish-white hair and darker facial bands. They were three days old – noisy in complaint and sucking greedily with their in-curved tongues – when Keely gave birth to triplets in a nest three holes away. Caileag was now at Ash Tree, which she was sharing with her yearling twins. She had three cubs, one of them stillborn, although she was not yet aware of it. In The

Corrach sett was a young boar – a wanderer in search of a mate.

The sows were slack-skinned and baggy as spring bears, and needed food; but during the first three days of their cubs' life they made only brief forays from the sett to dig in the oakwood leaf litter for roots, bluebell bulbs, crawlies or earthworms. When they uncovered woodlice, which Simon called slaters, they ignored them or scraped them aside. Sometimes they found acorns that had been buried by squirrels or jays.

When Caileag realised that one of her cubs was dead she carried it outside in her mouth, dug a hole while still holding it, and buried it, covering the grave with soil and withered leaves. At morning light, when all the badgers were below ground, The Corrach dog fox found the place, dug the cub from its grave, and carried it away.

Soon Mathair and Keely were foraging farther afield, digging and scraping in the oakwood and the glen, and visiting the grass moor on most nights to hunt for voles; but twice during each darkness they returned to the sett to suckle their cubs. Caileag was hunting in The Corrach or at the head of the glen, and they often met her there or on the grass moor. Three badgers hunting for voles left their marks. They clawed at the creeps, tearing the tussocks apart; they furrowed the ground and dug holes in it, seeking out sleeping nests. A few of the holes they used as latrines.

Each night Bodach held ceremony with Mathair and Keely – grappling, bouraching and setting scent on each other – and at some time he visited Caileag at Ash Tree, either before she left at darkening or after she was home in the morning. He was intolerant of the young boar at The Corrach and chased him when he saw him. But when Caileag's yearlings moved there, and settled with him, he became tolerant and accepted him as a member of the clan.

With the glen and all the low ground long clear of snow Bodach took the familiar trail to Drochaid, and one night, near the ride, he was attracted to a leaf-filled hole in a bank under the low-spreading branches of a big hawthorn. After scraping away the top layer of leaves he cocked his head in listening attitude, so perhaps he was hearing something. Then he began to dig in earnest, and syne he could smell hedgehog. The beast was hibernating, balled up and well padded with leaves, its breathing and heartbeats slowed down to near-death and its body temperature lowered, which is the difference between hibernation and mere long sleeping. In winter, badgers sleep for long periods but do not hibernate; hedgehogs sleep for months and do.

Bodach clawed the quilled beast from its bed, tore it open at the chink in its armour, and it was dead without waking or knowing anything about it. Although cooler than it would have been in summer or autumn the flesh was warm, and he ate all there was to eat, scraping the inside of the skin with his front teeth and leaving only the quilled jacket. At summer weight the hedgehog would have made a substantial meal; at winter's end it was a filler, not a gorge. So he still had the hunger gripe in his belly.

Cuffing the barbed skin aside he pushed through the fence to the tarmac road in the ride. It was filmed with ice no thicker than the water film on which whirligig beetles whirligig, so he did not skid. The ride was still cluttered with timber and building materials. Snow and frost had held up construction and only two of the cottages had roof timbers in place and sacking stacked to cover them. Remembering the dustbin at the workmen's hut Bodach went there and knocked it over, and this time found crusts of bread, a shallow tin that had contained steak and kidney pie, half a packet of potato crisps, a piece of fat bacon, and some apple cores. After emptying the bin he left the hut, skirting round some deep, open manholes, and followed the tarmac road to the farm bridge.

In the old stackyard was a roomy lean-to shed housing a Large White sow and eight piglets, warmly bedded on straw. The lean-to had a quarter door on the lee side, giving the grumphie and her family access to a half acre paddock, for Drummond was an unbeliever in hemming pigs in sties or crowding them in sweat boxes. For years he had reared pigs for his own use, with a few left over for private sale and the grumphie produced his baconers. She was huge and wise, friendly with Drummond and his son but a chaser of dogs and cats. Although Drummond did not know it she had once caught and eaten one of the half-grown tortoiseshell cats belonging to the farm.

Bodach climbed over netted fence into the paddock, attracted by the feeding trough outside the lean-to, and with no interest in piglets, although if he had found a dead one it is quite likely that he would have eaten it. The grumphie knew he was there before he got as far as the feeding trough and came lumbering out with her snout in the air, squealing in rage. Bodach, taken by surprise, hesitated for a moment, and her jaws almost reached him before he broke for the fence, with her teeth champing at his scut. She tried to reach him as he was climbing over the fence, but missed. She returned, grunting, to her plaintive piglets while Bodach, terrified as he had never been in his life, ran the tarmac road halfway to the larch wood before stopping to draw breath.

After a fortnight of sun and cloud, warmth and cold, rain, hail, sleet and refrigerated winds, spring came to the hill and the snow retreated towards Ben Dearg's crown. The white hares were blue again, and Fraioch the stoat moulted from white to brown. Tits flitted again in the alders along the Breac. Down at Drochaid, where Drummond was ploughing, peewits were wavering in bat-flight or throwing about the sky with the wind-song in their wings, whooping glad tidings of dry tilths and green days ahead.

One of Keely's cubs died when the crows in the oakwood were laying and Sealgair's mate sitting on five white eggs. Like Caileag, she carried it outside in her mouth and buried it in a shallow grave; no fox found it and it remained there. That left four cubs in the sett, now strong enough on their legs to play along the lateral tunnels, but not yet ready to view the world from their doorstep.

On a windy morning of clear sky, with a soaring lark crossing the T of a jet vapour trail, and woodpigeons croodling in the wood, a red vixen came prospecting along the frontage of the

Breac sett, with her ears up, her brush slack, and the life inside her stirring. She was prospecting, no more; near her time but not yet ready to go to ground. She favoured the hole from which Tarf had bolted a vixen the previous spring, scraped it clear of the leaves that blocked it, then walked cat-footed away, over-printing hindfoot on fore and leaving a single line of tracks.

Inevitably, Coll and Simon found her after she had moved in, because hill men will always look for a fox where they have found one before. Pharic had seen her earlier, on foot leaving the oakwood, but dismissed her from his mind when he saw her trotting away to the Ben Dearg scree.

'The bitch had to pick this place again, of course,' Coll said, with a resigned shake of his head. 'Why the hell do badgers put up with it?'

'I keep askin masel that,' Simon replied. 'Mind you, I think we could risk the dogs. The place looks like a single end tae me . . . well . . . at least we ken its blin on wan side. The same thing could hardly happen again as happened last year.'

'Hm-hm,' Coll said. 'I widna bet on it. No! I'm not risking the dogs in there again. If the damned badger popped up Tarf micht back off, but then again she micht get her wild up and argue. She's learned now to give holes a miss, but face to face . . . and being girned at . . . the temper would get the better of her, I'm sure . . .'

'So whit dae we dae?' Simon asked. 'Leave her be?'

'That'll be right,' Coll laughed. 'Mind you, I would if it was left to me. For that maitter so would Pharic, I'm sure. But it widna do. No! I'll sit up for her and shoot her.'

'And the cubs?'

'Dammit! If we could get the cubs I'd leave herself be. I've a book in the house where a chap suggests just that, and I'm inclined to agree.' A thought suddenly occurred to him. 'Dammit, Simon! We could let her oot, and keep her oot, then send Tarf in for the cubs. It would be the work of minutes, and no rumpus. She could be in and oot again without the badgers kenning she was there!'

'Suits me,' Simon agreed.

171

'I'll see Pharic tonight, and if he's agreeable that's what we'll do.'

The following morning they came by the sett on their way to the hill with Pharic to look at other fox dens. Coll had Tarf and Sionnach on leashes. Simon had with him an old terrier called Sandy, tied with a bit of climbing rope. They let all three poke their faces into the hole, and were amazed when none of them showed any great interest. They all wanted to be at the other holes.

'Looks like she's flitted,' Pharic observed.

'Could be,' said Coll, 'but I don't believe it.'

'Let me try Sandy,' Simon suggested. 'He's had donkey's years at it, and he'll come oot like a shot the minute he's cried on.'

Reluctantly Coll agreed. 'But get him out at the first sign of a rumpus! Thur dogs are foxhunters, not badgers' dinners.'

Simon slipped Sandy, an old Jack Russell with much scarred muzzle, and he went straight down without coaxing. The men waited, down on their knees, listening for his bark. There was none. Instead he was backing out, and when his head cleared the hole they saw he had a small black fox cub in his jaws. It was dead, cold and mutilated.

'God Almichty!' Simon exclaimed.

Coll took the cub from the dog, and he went in again. In a minute he was out with another cub.

'Jesus!' Pharic said. 'Now try and work that one out.'

Sandy brought out three more fox cubs, and went below a sixth time.

'There must be another one yet,' Coll observed. 'That'll mak six. A fair litter.'

But what Sandy came out with next was not a fox cub. It was a badger cub, about five weeks old, and it too was mutilated and cold. The men looked at each other. Pharic took off his two snooter and scratched his head. Coll sighed, in puzzlement.

'That's wan for the book,' Simon said, 'and dinna ask me tae read it!'

'She must have killed her cubs,' Pharic suggested.

'I don't believe that any more than I believe she deserted them,' said Coll. 'But I wonder what the hell's happened to her.'

'We'll never know that now,' said Pharic.

'I wonder what killed the badger cub,' Simon said to Coll.

'Not the badger, surely,' Coll replied. 'Any more than the fox killed hers. I wonder now . . .'

'What?' They looked at him.

'You'll think I'm daft for sure. But supposing – just supposing – the fox killed the badger cub. And supposing the badgers killed the fox cubs . . . They do sometimes, after all . . .'

'That leaves the vixen. Where has she got to?'

'If the badgers did kill her cubs, then likely she left,' said Coll. 'Seems to me to be the only reasonable explanation.'

They had to leave it at that.

The relationship between fox and badger has for long intrigued people who become intrigued with such things. There are those who believe that a badger will front for a fox lodger when the terriers are put in, whereas the beast is simply defending its own home. Many Masters of Foxhounds dislike the badger because they believe it is a routine killer of fox cubs, which it is not. That it kills fox cubs sometimes is a fact. If it was a routine killer of fox cubs Highland foxhunters would love it, which many of them do not; and vixens would soon stop whelping in badger setts.

Bodach learned something new about foxes when he was homing from the far side of The Corrach on a snell morning of overcast sky and frore. He had had a poor night. The lean times were not yet over, and there was hunger in him. In a birch thicket he clawed at vole creeps, but caught no vole. From there he shambled through blaeberry cushions into The Corrach pines – a shadow in the half-light of no shadows; a movement following a flicker of white. He was not wasting time, but not hurrying either, for daylight was yet some way off and the overcast sky would give him more badger time.

Ahead and around his nose found nothing to trouble him, and the morning sounds were reassuring to his ears: the stirring of small birds, the waking gutturals of crows, the hoot of The Corrach tawny owl, the gruff bark of Boc-earb. He plodded on seeking, turning aside to scrape at the lightly frosted ground, and sniff. In a grassy clearing he saw a rabbit – a big one – and it had a broken hind leg. It was grazing, dragging the leg. It broke away at his approach – stumbling, cavorting, falling and rising. Now the lumbering badger became all weasel, massively sinuous, bounding with rump high. A few bounds brought him alongside the rabbit, which rolled over on to its side, with the broken leg sticking up and waving like a feeble arm. It squealed when Bodach, turning short, reached for it; it squealed when he chopped, and the squeals set the crows talking in The Corrach.

Bodach carried the rabbit to the base of a big oak tree in a horseshoe of brown, withered fern stools. With his back against the tree he squatted down and began to eat, chewing through the neck and into the chest cavity, bloodying the white of his face while deftly turning back the skin with his foreclaws. An early risen crow, flapping overhead, saw the badger below and flew into the oak tree, *kraa-ing* his discovery. Standing tall, with his neck long, he peered down and saw what the badger was eating; he could also hear the cracking of bones. Bodach, ignoring him, went on breaking bones and peeling skin. The crow began to hop about on the branch, chortling hoarse comment and snipping off brittle twigs with his beak; he was waiting on, hoping for leavings, being a jackal to trade. Bodach continued to ignore him.

Then, suddenly, the crow's neutral comments changed to harsh caws of recognition, and Bodach's head came up. This was crow-talk that interested him.

Nothing came to his ears, but wind flaffs brought fox to his nose. The taint had little interest for him; he registered it, no more, and returned to his eating. But this fox was coming on, straight towards him, its scent becoming thicker by the second, almost filling his nostrils. He raised his head again, and presently even his poor eyes could make out two foxes – not one.

174

They were padding along flank to flank, light footed and wary; dog and vixen, with ears up and open forward; a mated pair with no family yet, hungry, and with time to spare.

Bodach looked at them speculatively, tilting his muzzle, bear-like: not afraid of them, nor alarmed, nor angry, but watchful for fox nonsense. The foxes closed in and sat down side by side at the open end of the horseshoe, like spectators – the dog with his tongue hanging from the side of his mouth, the vixen with her eyes slitted. They knew something about badgers, and what they knew made them ponder. They were great ponderers, singly or together, and they were in no hurry. Perhaps they knew Bodach was running out of time. Perhaps they also knew that he could not carry the rabbit home. Perhaps they knew that if he could not eat all of it he would walk away and leave some of it. Perhaps they knew no more than the crow, and like him were merely hoping.

So the three faced each other – the foxes pondering, the badger alert and on guard. Then the vixen rose, yawned, stalked a few paces round on Bodach's left side, and sat down again. The dog fox pulled in his tongue and watched her, with head skewed. Bodach watched both of them, with his white arrowhead flicking right and left.

The vixen rose again, and this time she disappeared behind some brushwood, still farther round on Bodach's left. Now he drew back hard against the trunk of the oak, leaving the rabbit remains exposed. First suspicions were forming, and he began to bristle; but he was still cool, peaceable, not truculent, minding his own business. He had withstood the confrontation; now he was working at the peace conference. The vixen broke it up. She whisked from behind her brushwood screen, rushed at him, said *Ach* to his face, snapped her teeth at him, then withdrew. It was over in two seconds: on stage, off stage, and no vixen to be seen. But Bodach would not be drawn by mock threat, however provocative. Now he knew what they were after. He pulled the rabbit behind him and sat on it!

He was rocking like a bear now, with his eyes on the dog fox and his nose on the vixen. When his nose lost her he knew she was round behind him; but he had the oak tree at his back so did not make the mistake of turning his head to look for her. Still he faced forward, making no threatening move. Grumbling growls betrayed his mounting annoyance, but he was not yet roused, and it would need more than had happened to bring him to anger. The crow was now craning forward on his perch, yarring droll commentary; but he was beginning to realise there was nothing here for him, and syne he flew away to join two others flapping overhead against the brightening sky.

The peace conference in the horseshoe was now over, and again it was the vixen that made the first war-like move. She flashed round suddenly on Bodach's right flank, clicked her teeth at his ear, and turned away again, with perfect coordination of footwork and rudder. Yet she had almost made a mistake. Bodach could not match her footwork or her pace, but he could strike like a viper. Although she had taken him by surprise he was countering as she swerved, and his teeth snapped on the hair tips of her ruff. That made her cautious. She drew back snarling, and faced him in full view, with head lowered and brush slack. The dog fox was now on his feet, staring at the badger with expressionless amber eyes. Bodach flicked his arrowhead from one to the other. The vixen probed forward with a raised forepaw and bared her teeth at him. She leered at him. But he had blunted her edge, and now she was warming to the two fox game – taunting to draw him away from the rabbit, while her mate moved in to snatch it.

Bodach was becoming uneasy about his bed time; only the overcast sky was holding back the light. A cock pheasant was crowing; cushats were flying out of the wood. A wren flew from a fern stool and whirred past the vixen's face. Bodach knew he would soon be caught in daylight; only hunger was holding him. Two choices were open to him. He could walk away and go home, leaving the rabbit; or he could take it with him. If he carried it away he would have the foxes snapping at his heels, tormenting and delaying him, and there would be no peace to eat it. Either way he would lose it. To carry it home, and into the sett, would have been a breach of all badger tradition, and the thought never entered his head. He had to eat it where he stood, if he was to eat it at all, and that meant holding off the foxes.

He chose to fight.

With disconcerting speed he launched at the dog fox, taking him by surprise and snapping off a mouthful of neck fur; but the fox, light of foot and quick as any weasel, was in his stride before he was hit by forty pounds of bone and muscle, backed up by teeth like a trap. He ran until Bodach's rush was spent, then turned about and came mincing back, still fit and willing to play the two fox game. He had a bare patch on his neck, hardly bigger than his eye, but the skin was uncut so he was probably unaware of the loss.

Now Bodach rushed at the vixen. She leaped aside and, before he could turn, the dog fox was snapping at his scut. When he leaped at the dog fox, the vixen sneaked in behind him to snatch up the rabbit. She got her teeth in it, but dropped it at the pick-up when Bodach, suspecting what she was doing, twisted about and almost caught her by a foot. He was on the boil now, and dangerous. He picked up the rabbit and backed with it against the tree. He had no answer to the foxes, and time was on their side. When he tried to eat they closed in and taunted him together, and all he could do was hold them off. The tactics that would have worked against one fox were useless against two; and these were a quick-witted pair, nimble and not much afraid, and hungry and determined forby.

It was at this point in the stalemate that Boc-earb arrived.

The foxes backed away when he came rampaging into the horseshoe – touzy in the moult but clean-antlered, with the spring in his knee and the glitter in his eye. His intrusion was inexplicable and beyond reasonable expectation; but he was there, and real. He came with his chin down, and his ivory top tines pointing like twin dirks at the foxes. He went through the ritual of scooping in the grass with a forehoof, then he buckled at the knees and charged them, with his head down to his knees and his dirks striking upwards.

They could read the signs and were not there when he reached where they had been. They were away at speed, leaping

177

high, and separating to right and left. Boc-earb did not chase. He faced about and grunted at Bodach, then minced twice round the horseshoe, stopping at every other stride to stamp with a forehoof or rip the fern stolls with his antlers. When Bodach picked up his rabbit to go he turned his back on him, and stood taut, with his ears up, staring in the direction taken by the foxes. And he saw them . . .

Thrawn as ever, they were skulking back on converging trails, alert for tantrums from the buck but interested mainly in Bodach's rabbit. What was driving Boc-earb no one can guess, or is anyone's guess. He was behaving as though he had his fires stoked for the rut, which was as far ahead as it was behind. Perhaps some experience with foxes in the past had turned him into a feuding savage. Whatever the reason, he went bounding out of the horseshoe the moment he saw the pair, passed Bodach with his rabbit, and charged down on the vixen.

She turned at once and fled, but this time he followed her, and he was treading hard on her heels when she ducked under a windfall out of his reach. He leaped over it, then stotted about, seeking her, like a dog that has lost a rabbit in tall cover. He leaped back over the windfall, saw the dog fox running, and gave chase. The fox headed for the birch thicket, with head down and brush flying, running at full stretch, and was into the cover before Boc-earb reached the edge. The buck's nostrils were flared and his flanks heaving; he was blowing and showing his tongue. But the fire was still in him, and he vented his rage thrashing brushwood with his antlers. For some minutes he stared in the direction taken by the foxes; then he relaxed, lowered his head, and began to graze in the horseshoe.

Bodach carried his rabbit from The Corrach as far as Ash Tree fork, where he squatted down to eat it. Caileag, returning to her cubs, arrived while he was still eating, and whether because he had eaten all he wanted, or was sharing, he left the remains to her and set off for Breac at a swinging trot.

Chapter Sixteen

The night was clear, with the hedgerow trees tossing in the wind, and the moon a goblin's mirror above Drochaid Farm, where everybody was abed and the collie Nell asleep in the hay.

At one o'clock in the morning a dark shape detached itself from the shadows of the kitchen garden hedge and hopped along the tarmac road towards the larch wood. The hopping shape was a brown hare, with distended flanks and the moon glint in her eye. At the last cottage – still doorless, windowless and unroofed – she turned left into the old cornfield, now sealed off from cattle, where the young grass would be left to grow on to be cut for hay. There was no cover in the field for a hare, so she hopped across it, side by side with her own bobbing shadow, to the hedgerow where there were tangles, heaps of old straw and tussocks of bleached grass. The hare found a tussock that suited her and pressed out a bed in it.

Two hours later she left it, and sat upright in the open, with her long ears erect and her cleft nostrils sifting the wind. A tawny owl whooped suddenly in the ride and she lent an ear to him; the other she directed to the inbye where sheep were moving. But she still kept her nose to the wind.

Presently she took a great leap sideways; then another; and yet another. She was breaking her scent line. After the third leap she hopped away from the hedgerow into the open hayfield, with bobbing, rocking-horse movements, to crop grass down-wind from the tussock. She was keeping check on what she had hidden there. In the tussock, which was well sheltered to windward, were three tiny leverets, open-eyed, with wavy silken fur. They were crouched side by side, moveless and silent, patiently awaiting the return of the doe.

The tawny owl from the ride flew low over the pasture, on muffled wings, his round eyes scanning the ground and his ears alert for the slightest sound. The hare tensed when she saw his wavering ground shadow, and when he whooped she started forward, fearing for her leverets. She was young, new to the experience of motherhood, and nervous. But her leverets were safe from the owl; he could neither see nor hear them. He flew from the hayfield, and she resumed her grazing.

Suddenly six sheep burst through the fence from the inbye, obviously put on foot by something they feared. The thud of their hooves brought the hare's ears up, and when she saw they were running in the direction of the tussock she leaped out to head them. She turned them, as a collie would have done, baring her big yellow teeth. Not that she could, or would, have done anything with them; baring them was an expression of anger and alarm and no threat to the sheep. The sheep milled round, startled, then broke away from the apparition that smelled like a hare but acted like a dog.

An hour later the hare returned to her leverets, approaching the tussock warily, and breaking her scent line by great sideways leaps and back-tracking. Once she was settled in the clump the leverets snuggled against her and nursed greedily. They drowsed, and fell asleep. Soon afterwards the hare drew away from them, and left the tussock, going through her leaping ritual as before.

Fox smell on the wind half an hour later brought her upright in alarm, with ears erect and nostrils twitching. The smell came to her in elusive whiffs – wind-scattered, intermittent, yet very real and menacing. Presently she placed him upwind from her leverets; he was casting across, with the wind ruffling his fur. He had no information about her leverets, and padded on and away out of sight and smell. The hare grazed again, with her nose alert for any taint of fox on the wind. The fox did not return, but another prowler arrived, down wind, following the hedge line – a badger.

Bodach plodded along the endrigg, his white arrowhead heralding his coming, and the hare, watching, wondered. Normally she paid no heed to badgers; but this beast was moving dangerously – stolidly, accidentally, but none the less dangerously – towards the tussock that held her leverets. So once again she acted, in the only way she knew – by harrying. She knew she could never induce him to chase her; but she might divert him from his route by hustling and chivvying him, and breaking through his armour plating of thrawn calm.

So she rushed at him; she leaped at him; she leaped over him. She actually kicked him in the face with her big hairy hindfeet; but not a second time, because the snap of his jaws had been swift and menacing. All her harrying and tormenting failed to turn Bodach from his chosen route, which after all was his own, and he bored on, grunting his displeasure at her unprovoked attack. All he wanted was to be left alone to go his own way.

In a frenzy now the hare rushed at him, with her teeth bared. She might as well have threatened the farm tractor. Bodach lumbered on, grunting and shaking his head, straight for the tussock where three leverets were sleeping: three leverets that had yet to see their first daylight. He was twelve feet from the tussock, with head down, and plodding on, when the hare rushed at him from the hedgebottom, close to his face, and he turned after her to snap at her. He darted at her – three paces, then four; then swung back to his trail. By then he was upwind from the tussock, and he padded on, not knowing the leverets were there.

The wind died, and the frost settled; by morning there would be cranreuch. Bodach hunted the hayfield hedgerow, then crossed the inbye to the cottages; the sheep were now on the tarmac road, heading for the farm. He followed the inbye fence to the garden and climbed in. Before he left he had dug three great holes in the herbaceous border, and eaten part of the roots of three clumps of Drummond's lupins. In one of the holes he left dung; signing his name to the work as Drummond described it later. Outside the garden Nell was waiting for him.

She had been awakened by the sheep trotting into the closs, and after pushing them into the rootfield, which was the best she could do, she had winded Bodach and tracked him to the garden. There was little of the puppy left in Nell now, and although she had not yet developed the hill dog's hostile suspicion of everything on four legs except sheep, she decided the badger should not be there and meant to send him on his way.

When she rushed at him, flashing her teeth, Bodach bolted; he had no quarrel with Nell and his one thought was to get away from her. Having no long-used, familiar trail through the building site he had to look and think where he was going, and she made it difficult for him by heading him, flanking him, tailing him, forcing him to keep changing direction. Here was no kinaesthetic sense; he was running blind. The pile of big concrete pipes loomed ahead of him and he porpoised towards it – into a manhole. He fell six and a half feet into six inches of watery earth and cement.

Nell stopped at the manhole, looked down at him, then leaped and reared, growling and barking; but after fifteen minutes she realised he was not coming out, so she lost interest and trotted back to the farm. Bodach reared against the brick walls of his prison, clawing and sclaffing, churning water, earth and cement into grey ooze with his hindfeet. His belly and legs were plastered and syne, trying to jump, he fell on his side, rolled over on to his back when trying to rise, and slaigert himself to the neck. The mud was cold, and he became hot with his exertions. When he backed against one of the walls to rest he felt the cold travelling up his legs. Above him the frost was keen, but no ice formed in the manhole because of his trampling. At first light he was sitting in the ooze, exhausted and shivering.

He heard the voices of the men when they arrived for work in the morning, and Drummond's tractor on the tarmac road. The fields were white, and the trees and hedgerows rimed. In the hayfield rooks were stabbing and dibbling, glossed like beetles in the morning sun, swinging their ragged kilts, their eyes like ripe elderberries peering over yashmaks of grey skin. Wood-pigeons were also down in the field, bosomy and buxom, with smooth pates and not a feather out of place: like mechanical toys tilting forward to peck with yellow and vermilion beaks – white-necked, pomaded hyacinth blue and salmon pink in the morning sun. Starlings formed cloud and pitched, like blowflies on a carcass, and the white field was stippled with restless, bustling dots, seeking the same apparent nothing as the rooks and the woodpigeons.

Nell saved Bodach's life.

Following Drummond on the tractor, she remembered the badger in the manhole, and sneaked away to find out if it was still there. It was; and she announced her re-discovery in a frenzy of barking that attracted the attention of a carpenter who came to see what all the noise was about.

'Whit hae ye got in there, wummin?' he said to Nell. She wagged her tail, and looked into the manhole with her head half cocked as though expecting him to do something about it. The man looked in and saw Bodach, curled in a corner, plastered and miserable, and shivering in distress. Even the white arrow-head of him was coated in grey mud.

'Haw, Jimmy!' the carpenter called to a mate. 'There's something in this manhole the dug's at. You better fetch the gaffer. It looks like a bliddy panda tae me.'

Drummond left the tractor and arrived at the manhole before the foreman. He called Nell to heel and looked in.

'It's a badger,' he announced. 'Now hoo the hell did it get in there? Looks kinna far gaun tae me, and nae wunner if it's been in there maist o the nicht. You chaps haud on here and I'll gang tae the ferm and phone the verra man that'll sort this lot oot.

Nell! Come in ahint!' Nell fell to heel and followed him to the tractor.

Coll and Simon arrived in the Land Rover and backed it up to the manhole. When Coll looked down at the trapped badger he shook his head.

'Looks fair connacht to me, poor brute,' he said. 'We'll need a bit rope, and a pair of kitchen steps, and a strong hessian bag, although I don't think this one'll have any argument left in it.'

Simon drove Drummond to the farm in the Land Rover, and presently they returned with step ladder, rope and a hessian bag. Coll placed the ladder in the manhole, wedging the bottom securely. He made a noose at one end of the rope and handed the other to Drummond.

'Are you going down?' Drummond asked. 'It's a bit risky, is it not?'

'I doubt it,' Coll assured him. 'When I've got the noose on the beast's neck, I'll ask you to pull. Then pull! But steadily. I want the beast to walk up if it can. And you, Simon, have the bag ready.'

'I'll gie him a bit haun,' the carpenter offered.

'Just watch you don't gie a bit haun tae the chap in the hole,' Simon laughed.

Coll climbed down the steps, and stood in the sludge, which lapped almost to the top of his veldtschoen boots. Bodach bored into a corner, with his nose tucked against his chest, aware of the man but with no thought of defending himself, or offering resistance. There was still body heat and latent strength in him, but no fight. Coll forced the noose down between the arrowhead and the wall; then up round the thick neck. Winding the slack of the rope round his right hand he pulled Bodach as gently as he could to the bottom of the steps and hoisted him until his front feet were on the bottom rung. He passed the slack up to Drummond and called:

'Now pull! But slowly.'

Drummond strained on the rope, and Coll pushed Bodach from behind. Helped by the rope, which he hardly felt round his neck, and feeling the wooden step under his feet, he managed to claw his way from rung to rung, supported by Coll's hands on his rump. Simon and the carpenter held the sack open at the top of the steps and Coll, following Bodach, pushed him into it. Simon took out his gralloching knife and cut through the rope at the back of Bodach's head, then tied the neck of the sack.

'Now,' Coll said to him, 'we'd better get yokit and get this beast home. It's in pretty bad shape.' To Drummond he said: 'We'll do the best we can for it. Thank you, and thank all you chaps for your help.'

Bodach would certainly have died had he been left in the manhole for another twenty-four hours, or less; he could not have remained standing for very much longer, and lying down in six inches of near-freezing sludge would quickly have drained his body heat. But he was not as far down as Coll thought, despite his present indifference about what was happening to him. It was this indifference that made him much easier to handle than they had expected, although he might well have behaved no differently in a trap or confined, showing no more aggression than a trapped wolf. But nobody in his senses takes careless risks with a badger's teeth.

'The first thing is to get this damned muck off him,' Coll told Simon. 'If we don't it'll harden like cement, and likely there's cement in it anyway, and he'll be left like a bliddy hedgehog. That's if he survives.' Coll had already noticed that the badger was a boar.

He ran his hand on Bodach's plastered back, against the lie of the hair, and saw that the underfur was dry and mostly clean. He also felt the body warmth through it, and that made him more optimistic.

'You know, Simon, come to think of it . . . Drummond's dog . . . now if she hadna drawn attention this beast could still be there in yon manhole . . .'

'Aye! And if Drochaid hadna been there himsel it micht be there yet. He didna let ony grass grow below his feet.' Simon lapsed into a local habit of sometimes identifying a farmer by calling him by the name of his farm.

'Well, anyway, we'll hose the beast down from head to tail. That should get the muck off him without wetting him through. We'll use the garden hose, the one with the spray, and attach it to the mixing tap in the kitchen. Will it stretch this far?'

'Och, yes!' Simon said. 'I've had it further'n this. I'll gang and fix it up.'

'Yes, do that, and I'll go fetch two-three bales of good straw. A warm bed's what's needed, then we can leave him to dry out and get the blood moving again. Unless maybe he gets pneumonia whatever.'

'Aye. Aiblins that could happen. It'll be that hypothermia they talk aboot that's the bother wi him.'

When they had the hose fixed, set for fine spraying, Simon roped Bodach again and stood him in the middle of the concrete floor of the kennel enclosure. Coll sprayed him from head to tail, then round his legs and under his belly, with water at a little over blood heat. The sludge flowed from him in a thick stream. When they had washed him clean, with even the face of him white again, they removed the rope and footed him gently but firmly, one on each side, into the great pile of straw Coll had put in the kennel. Bodach burrowed into the heart of it, and curled up, with his muzzle between his forepaws. Later Coll put in a rabbit, some dog biscuit, a dish of milk and a bowl of water, and said to Simon: 'We'll see gin tomorrow morning how he is, but for now we'll leave him be. There's nothing more we can do for him.'

Pharic came round next morning, before leaving for the hill, and the three men went to the kennel. The rabbit was gone and the milk dish empty; only one dog biscuit was missing.

'That's a good sign, anyway,' he said to the others. 'A beast that's really sick winna eat.'

Pharic laughed. 'You know, there's been mair badgers than dugs in this kennel in the past twelvemonth. Are you for having a look at your invalid?' he asked Coll.

'Indeed yes!' He bent over the heap and began to pull away

straw with his stick. Then he stopped suddenly, listening, and smiled. 'Listen to this!' he said to the others. 'He's snoring away in there like a contented pig!'

They listened and heard. Coll rose to his feet.

'We won't bother him any more just now, then,' he said. 'Looks like he's going to be all right. But we'll keep him another day, to let him feed up and warm himself through.'

'Are you ettling to keel this one too?' Pharic asked.

'Why not?' said Coll.

'Well, make it red this time,' Simon suggested. 'Then we'll ken the difference between him and the ither wan.'

'Blue is all I have,' said Pharic.

'Drochaid keels red,' Simon reminded him. 'We can get some there.'

'I'll get some red from Drochaid then,' Pharic offered, 'and daub him before we let him go. Byt the way,' he said to Coll, 'did I hear you say something about taking the loons and the lassies from the school out some night to see badgers?'

'Yes. During the Easter holiday. I fixed it with yon Miss Lindsay. Why?'

'Why not have them up to see this one before you turn it loose?'

'That's a good idea. But it would have to be after school, surely . . .'

'Maybe not,' Simon said. 'The heidmaister's a reasonable chap and very keen on the nature study. It's mair than likely he'll make it official – ye ken? Wan o thur field study things . . .'

'Right,' said Coll. 'I'll give him a ring on the phone and ask him. But it'll have to be tomorrow some time. I don't want to keep the beast here any longer than need be.'

'Well, I'm for off,' said Pharic. 'I'll get the stuff from Drochaid and keel this beast later on the day and get done wi it.'

Next afternoon Miss Lindsay arrived with eight children, including carrot head and the girl with the Titian hair.

'This is the Badger Group,' she told the stalkers.

'Badger group?' Coll was puzzled.

Simon laughed. 'They don't look much like badgers tae me,' he said.

'They've formed a badger study group,' Miss Lindsay explained. 'They'll be working on a badger project after Easter. They're so much looking forward to going out with you one night during the holiday. We could fix the night now if it suits you.'

'Better to wait and see what the weather says,' said Coll. 'That's what'll decide the night.'

He took the party into the kennel enclosure and closed the door. Then he went in and uncovered Bodach. The children exclaimed 'Oh!' Bodach was asleep, with a forepaw over his nose.

'Is that bluid on its neck?' carrot head asked.

'No!' Simon grinned at him. 'It's a keel mark, like on the sheep. There's another one in the glen keeled blue on the rump. If we get another one the shepherd's gaun tae keel it white. An what'll that gie us?'

After a moment's silence carrot head called out: 'Red, white and blue, sir!'

'That would be going over the score,' Coll said. 'Don't mind him, you chaps. I suppose you've been told how the beast cam to be here?'

'Yes, sir!' they sang out. 'It fell in a manhole!'

'That's right, and would have died if he'd been left there. We got him out, but it was the Drochaid collie . . .'

'Sir,' the girl with the Titian hair interrupted. 'Hamish Campbell says . . .' She hesitated.

'Yes?' Coll coaxed her quietly. 'Hamish Campbell says . . .?'

'He says his father says . . . his father says . . . he would have knocked it on the head . . . his father says some folk must have little to do to be bothering . . .'

'Well,' Coll broke in gently, 'we won't be knocking this one on the head.' He stroked Bodach's rump. 'I don't think he would like it, do you?'

'No, sir,' the girl agreed.

'It's not a nice thing to be clouted on the head, is it?'

'No, sir.'

'You were going to say something?' he addressed carrot head.

'Yes, sir. The postman fell on Hogmanay nicht and dunted his heid. They had to put stitches in it.'

'That's right!' Simon said. 'It can happen to the best o us. Postie's a grand chap and his heid's feeling it yet. There's ithers though,' he went on with some heat, 'whase heids button up the back and they're no that far from . . .'

'Excuse me,' Miss Lindsay broke in. 'Could you perhaps tell us why badgers have white stripes on their faces?'

Simon pointed to Coll, who thought for a moment, then said: 'Folks that study these things reckon it's a warning pattern for other beasts to get out of the way, and that seems likely enough to me. The one thing you'll see about a badger on the darkest night is its face.'

'Are they vicious, then?'

'No, I wouldn't say that. I'd say vicious applies only to people, to us. This beast is a wild animal, and frightened, and he's been through a hard time. Look at him. Would you like to stroke him?' he asked the children.

'Ye-es!' they called out in chorus.

'Quiet, then! And gentle! But hold on a minute!' he pulled some straw over Bodach's head and shoulders. 'Covering up the business end of him just in case,' he explained to Miss Lindsay. 'I don't think he'll try to bite, but you never can tell.'

One at a time the children knelt and patted Bodach lightly on the rump. He dozed on.

For the first time the boy with the dark sheemach head and the blue eyes spoke: 'How long do badgers live?' he asked.

'If they've got the same number o lives as a cat,' Simon told him, 'this one's used up eight o them!'

'They reckon,' Coll was smiling, 'that if a beast gets to its second year it should live as long as a dog . . . say . . . twelve . . . maybe up to fifteen years . . . barring accidents. Like falling into a manhole, and naebody there . . .'

'Or crossing the . . .' Simon began, then stopped.

189

After the children had gone Coll said to Simon:

'Pharic's coming round later, before we turn this chap loose. I'd like to gang to the Breac sett before then. It's likely he'll mak straight for hame, and if hame's where we think it is I should see him syne.'

'You want him turned loose at the badger gate?'

'I think so; just on darkening. I'll be in place by then. Put him down inside the gate, with the open end of the sack pointing for home. Let him take his time coming out. Don't spill him.'

'Message understood,' Simon said.

Coll was seated in his favourite oak tree half an hour before darkening. Sealgair the tawny owl was already on the wing, hunting along the Breac; a woodcock appeared in the clearway of sky and presently Coll could hear him croaking and chirping on his roding, eve-flight. Mathair and Keely came out when the light was fading. They nosed over the mounds, shambled halfway to the Breac, then came back to scratch near their tunnels. Mathair lay down when two small arrowheads appeared at the entrance to her tunnel, and the cubs came out timidly to climb over her and bite playfully at her face. At another hole Coll saw two more white faces, but they withdrew almost at once and did not come out again.

Mathair rose, shook herself free of her cubs, and watched them go to ground; then she wandered away along the frontage of the sett, turned uphill and disappeared, and Coll thought she had gone for the first part of the night. But minutes later he saw two white faces coming towards him – two badgers rearing and grappling, and mounting each other in obviously friendly greeting. One of them was Mathair; the other was Bodach. Keely appeared from behind Coll's tree, and the three began to play – chasing each other up, down and across the slope, thudding among the oaks and crashing in the undergrowth.

Coll was thinking to himself that if ever there was a welcome home this was one. He expected all three to leave at any moment, but when the play was over, and Mathair and Keely trotted away to hunt, Bodach did not follow. He padded to his mound, stood there for a few seconds, sniffing the air, with his back to Coll, then went to ground. Coll waited for another half hour before climbing down from his tree. He lit his pipe and walked to the mound at the entrance to Bodach's tunnel. He knelt down and spoke into it.

'Keep oot o manholes in future. You're safer in the wan you're in.'